D1008540

Humble Pies
and White Lies

Elizabeth Penney

Annie's®

AnniesFiction.com

Humble Pies and White Lies
Copyright © 2017 Annie's.

All rights reserved. No part of this publication may be reproduced, stored in a retrieval system, or transmitted in any form or by any means—electronic, mechanical, photocopying, recording or otherwise—without the prior written permission of the publisher. The only exception is brief quotations in printed reviews. For information address Annie's, 306 East Parr Road, Berne, Indiana 46711-1138.

The characters and events in this book are fictional, and any resemblance to actual persons or events is coincidental.

Library of Congress-in-Publication Data
Humble Pies and White Lies/ by Elizabeth Penney
p. cm.
I. Title
2016955472

AnniesFiction.com
(800) 282-6643
Amish Inn Mysteries™
Series Creator: Shari Lohner
Series Editor: Lorie Jones
Cover Illustrator: Kelley McMorris

10 11 12 13 14 | Printed in China | 9 8 7 6 5 4 3 2 1

"The higher we are placed, the more humbly we should walk."

-Marcus Tullius Cicero

1

Friday before Thanksgiving

Liz Eckardt opened the old cookbook with reverence. For as long as she could remember, her mother had relied on this favorite edition to create delicious, memorable meals.

And now, hosting Thanksgiving at the Olde Mansion Inn, she hoped to do the same for her guests. For the former Boston attorney, buying an inn in the lovely small town of Pleasant Creek, Indiana, hadn't only marked a change of career. It had been a journey of discovering her Amish heritage and relatives, a blessed and heartwarming experience. Even if her godson, Steve, stationed in Kosovo, wouldn't make it home for the holiday, at least she had relatives nearby.

She flipped through the pages, selecting recipes and noting the ingredients she needed to purchase. Ron and Connie Gregg had reserved rooms for themselves and four adult children, making a total of six at Thanksgiving dinner. A decent-size turkey would feed at least twelve. *Oh, well, I'll eat the leftovers.* Liz favored turkey sandwiches with mayonnaise, cranberry sauce, and stuffing. Her stomach gurgled at the thought, and she laughed. After finishing this task, she would eat lunch.

The kitchen extension rang. "Good morning, Olde Mansion Inn. How may I help you?"

"Um, I was wondering if you have any rooms available tonight through Thanksgiving," a woman said tentatively. "If so, I'd like to book two."

How perfect. "Actually, I do have two rooms left. Shared bath, though, if that's all right. Are you coming to town for our big event?"

"Big event?" Her caller sounded puzzled.

"The inn is part of the first annual A Pleasant Creek Thanksgiving." The chamber of commerce's promotion included a variety of events starting the weekend before the holiday. "I'm offering a home-cooked Thanksgiving dinner as part of my holiday package."

"That sounds nice."

"Do you have family in the area? We can provide dinner for them too." Liz mentally enlarged the size of the turkey she would buy.

The caller was silent. "No, no family," she finally said. "I—we'll be there on business."

Now she was puzzled. *A business trip over Thanksgiving? What kind of company makes employees do that?* But two rooms booked meant a full house.

After reserving the rooms, Liz finished the main meal part of the menu. Next she considered dessert. Some people branched out into cakes, puddings, and cookies, but she preferred classic pies. Pumpkin, of course, and pecan and apple . . . A thought struck. Liz could bake a decent pie, but why serve decent when she could buy the best ever?

A moment later she crossed the central rotunda and entered Sew Welcome, the fabric store located inside the inn. Store partners Mary Ann Berne and Sadie Schwarzentruber were chatting with Caitlyn Ross, a friend and fellow member of the Material Girls quilting group.

"Good morning." Mary Ann smiled in greeting. As always, she

was immaculately groomed, every shiny strand of her silver shoulder-length bob in place. "Are you ready for the Thanksgiving festival?"

Liz joined them. "Almost. I just found out I have a full house for the week."

"That's great news." Caitlyn, cute and quirky with her red-streaked hair, pierced nostril, and tiny butterfly tattoo, was an emergency room nurse.

"You better hope there isn't an increase in accidents with all the visitors in town, Caitlyn," Sadie muttered. Tall, with white hair and sharp blue eyes, Sadie prided herself on her strong opinions and forthright manner. "I'm always so busy at Thanksgiving, and now we have this event to contend with."

"Look at it this way," Mary Ann said. "We're starting the Christmas shopping season a week earlier. That's good news for our bottom line."

Liz felt a pang of concern. "Do you still have time to make pies to sell, Mary Ann? I remember you did that last year." Mary Ann baked the best pies—with the flakiest crusts—she had ever eaten.

"Of course I do." Mary Ann picked up a clipboard and a pen. "Tell me what you need."

As Liz placed her order, an attractive dark-haired young woman wandered into the store, gazing around in curiosity. She had bright green eyes that stood out against her tan complexion, no doubt endowed by a salon rather than sunshine at this time of year.

"That's Tiffany Blake," Caitlyn said. "I went to school with her." She waved at her friend. "I didn't know you quilted, Tiff."

She drifted closer, still scanning the store. "I don't. But my therapist thought it'd be good for me to learn."

Liz exchanged glances with Mary Ann.

Sadie drew herself up, as though girding herself, but her tone was kind when she said, "We do have beginner classes. Would you like to sign up?"

"Sure, I'd love to." Tiffany wrote her name and phone number on the piece of paper Sadie practically placed under her nose.

"We're still firming up the arrangements, but we'll contact you with the date and time." Sadie tucked the sheet in a folder.

"I hope the classes are at night. I work at Stevens' Motors during the day. Right now I'm on my break." Tiffany glanced at the wall clock. "And I'd better get back."

Caitlyn snapped her fingers. "I thought I saw you in the office the other day. I refinanced my car through the low-interest loan special you were offering."

Tiffany placed her hand on her chest. "Not me. My boss, you mean."

"Whatever." Caitlyn rolled her eyes. "Anyway, there's a problem. I got another bill on my old loan, which I shouldn't have, right?"

Tiffany shrugged. "It must be a glitch. Come in and have Ms. Stevens look at it."

After Tiffany sashayed out, Caitlyn groaned. "I can't believe I have to run over there again. You know how you do something you think is a good idea, but somehow it screws everything up?"

"I certainly do." Liz thought of a plumbing improvement that had proven to be a nightmare when executed. *The joys of inn ownership.*

"I'm surprised. Stevens' Motors has an excellent reputation," Mary Ann said. "In fact, my car is being repaired there as we speak. I've known the owner, Claudia Stevens, for years."

"I've known her as long as you have, and, believe me, she isn't the easiest person to get along with." Sadie winked at Liz. "Ask Jackson. He'll agree." Jackson Cross was a local business owner and the mayor of Pleasant Creek.

Liz's interest was piqued. She and Jackson were good friends and had gone on a few low-key dates. "Why do you say that?"

"Claudia ran for mayor against Jackson in the last election." Sadie shook her head. "She didn't really have a chance, but she did her best to try to discredit him." She lowered her voice. "Worse, she took over her ex-husband's family dealership during the divorce. Many people think Bob got a raw deal."

"That's enough. Remember, this is a no-gossiping zone." Mary Ann's tone was teasing.

Sadie grumbled a reply, then went to help a customer browsing among the fabric bolts.

"Anyway, on another note, Claudia is sponsoring a pumpkin pie Baking Bonanza during the festival, and the winner gets to go to America Loves Pies, the national contest." Mary Ann smiled. "I can't wait."

"You're entering the Baking Bonanza?" Liz felt guilty for ordering three pies. Didn't Mary Ann have enough to do already?

"You bet she is," Sadie called out. "Her pumpkin pie is to die for."

The customer she was waiting on grinned. "I love pumpkin pie."

Mary Ann wagged a finger at Liz. "Don't even think about canceling your order. I want to do those pies for your guests."

"If you're sure . . ."

"I am. I might be up until midnight baking every night between now and Thanksgiving, but everyone is going to get their pies."

"Gee, that makes me feel better." Liz laughed.

Mary Ann waved a hand dismissively. "The Baking Bonanza is on Monday, and I'll be making Thanksgiving pies next Tuesday and Wednesday. Piece of cake."

"Piece of pie, you mean. Thanks again." Liz headed toward the door. "I'll let you ladies get back to work."

A man and a woman appeared in the doorway, looking confused. The woman was tall, blonde, and slender with pretty features, and the man was handsome and of Asian descent. They both wore black from head to toe.

"This is the Olde Mansion Inn, right?" the woman asked. "Where can I find the office?"

Sadie shrieked, "Piper Reynolds! What are you doing here?" She descended on the newcomer like a schooner in full sail.

Piper Reynolds was the guest Liz had booked a short while ago. But her impression had been that Piper didn't know anyone in town.

Sadie grabbed one of Piper's hands in both of hers. "Welcome to Pleasant Creek. We're so happy to see you."

Liz glanced at Mary Ann, whose face mirrored her own confusion. Caitlyn appeared focused on the young man, who was smiling at her.

"Piper is the host of *Taste and Tour*," Sadie gushed. "Don't you watch that show? Everyone does." She turned back to the television personality. "I loved the show featuring New Orleans crawfish gumbo. And the one where you tried the Vermont cheeses."

"Thanks so much," Piper said.

"Are you here for something special?" Sadie asked. "Or just passing through?"

"Ms. Reynolds rented a room from me," Liz said. She thrust out her hand to shake Piper's—after Sadie finally released it. "Hi. I'm Liz Eckardt, the owner of the Olde Mansion Inn. Welcome."

"Nice to meet you, Liz. Thanks for putting us up on such short notice." Piper introduced the young man as her cameraman, Tony Lee. "Tony and I are here to film a segment for my show. We're covering the pumpkin pie Baking Bonanza."

Sadie flapped her hands in excitement, dancing up and down on her toes. "Are you serious? You're going to film our pie contest?

That's fantastic." She turned to Mary Ann. "You're going to be on national television."

Mary Ann blanched. "Oh, my. I had no idea."

"It was a last-minute thing," Piper admitted. "America Loves Pies contacted the head production office and told them about it. We needed something different for Thanksgiving, and here we are." She grimaced. "You can only do so many turkey features."

"Forget the turkeys," Sadie declared. "Bring on the pies. My friend is one of the best bakers in the county—no, the state. Wait, what am I saying? The country. She's a surefire winner."

"Cut it out, Sadie." Now Mary Ann's cheeks flamed. She nodded at Piper. "Anyway, nice to meet you."

"Same here." Piper glanced at Liz. "We're quite tired so . . ."

Liz kicked into innkeeper gear. "Let me show you to your rooms."

Tony grinned. "See you later, ladies."

"Later, Tony." Caitlyn flashed him a smile.

Someone has made a new friend. Liz smiled to herself as she ushered the pair into the lobby. She checked them in, then escorted them up to the third floor. "This is the Sunset Room," she said, opening the door to the west-facing room, which featured a pleasant mix of contemporary and antique furniture set off by bright artwork and cushions.

She opened the door to a similar room across the way. "And this is the—"

"Let me guess. The Sunrise Room." Tony stuck his head around the jamb. "I'll take it since I'm an early riser."

"So am I," Piper said, giving her colleague a teasing frown. She stepped into the Sunset Room. "But this is fine."

"You can watch the sun set over Jaynes Lake from up here." Liz pointed out the body of water visible from the window. "Now there is one drawback, Tony. I don't know if Piper mentioned it, but you'll have to share a bathroom." She held her breath, hoping this information wouldn't change his mind. Guests were used to having their own bathrooms, and while the second-floor rooms had private baths, there wasn't enough room on the third floor for two.

Tony shrugged. "At least you have indoor plumbing. We've been in some remote places where all they had were outhouses."

"Anything for a story, right?" Piper smiled. "This is lovely, Liz. We'll be fine up here."

Liz gave them the spiel about breakfast and afternoon coffee hour, then mentioned the Thanksgiving dinner she was cooking for the other guests. "I don't usually provide main meals, but if you're still here, you're welcome to join us."

"That sounds wonderful, but I'll probably drive to Chicago on Wednesday to see my family." Tony glanced at Piper. "That is, if my boss will give me the day off."

Piper put her hands on her hips. "Of course you can go. Quit trying to make me out to be a dictator." By the smile on her face, Liz guessed she was joking.

Tony bowed. "I'm your main minion, and I never forget it." With a laugh he headed down the stairs. "I'll go get our bags out of the rental car."

"Thanks, Tony," Piper said. She covered her mouth to stifle a yawn. "Can I trouble you for a cup of coffee? I'm exhausted."

"Of course. Come on and I'll brew a fresh pot." As Liz led the way, she heard a thunderous crash. *What was that?* Heart in her throat, she practically ran down the two flights of stairs.

Sadie popped out of the store entrance when they reached the foot of the stairs, which ended in the central rotunda. "Did you hear that crash?" The older woman trotted through the foyer.

Driven by curiosity, Liz followed, Piper at her heels. A second later, Mary Ann and Caitlyn joined them.

Out on the porch, Tony dropped the bags he was carrying. "There's an accident up the street."

The others crowded to the railing to look.

About a block away, a shiny new car had swerved into one of the huge, ancient oak trees bordering the street.

Mary Ann gasped. "That's Claudia Stevens. I recognize her car."

2

"Call 911. Ask for an ambulance." With that order, Caitlyn took the steps two at a time and sprinted toward the accident.

"I'm on it." Mary Ann pulled a cell phone out of her pocket and placed the call.

The others moved off the porch and along the sidewalk toward the scene.

"She's an emergency room nurse," Liz told Tony, who was watching Caitlyn in amazement.

"Good thing she's here," he said. "The driver looks hurt."

Wincing in sympathy, Liz saw the driver was slumped over the wheel. She said a quick prayer that her injuries weren't serious. Caitlyn had reached the site and was wrestling with the door handle.

Piper put a hand to her head. "Did Mary Ann say Claudia Stevens? That's the woman we were supposed to meet, Tony. She's in charge of the pie Baking Bonanza."

"You're right. I didn't make the connection at first." Tony shook his head. "I hope she'll be okay."

Up the street, a siren sounded and a police vehicle hurtled into view, followed by a fire truck, also sounding its siren. Someone else on the street must have witnessed the accident and phoned it in.

"What a quick response time," Piper said. "I can't believe they're here already."

"I know, right?" Tony glanced at his boss. "In the city, they take forever."

"They're sending an ambulance," Mary Ann said, disconnecting as she caught up, huffing for breath.

A fireman and Chief Stan Houghton were helping Caitlyn open the door. To Liz's relief, the driver, an attractive middle-aged woman with short, styled hair, sat upright and started talking.

Sadie clutched Liz's arm. "Thank goodness. I think she's all right."

"It looks that way." Liz patted her friend's hand. Despite Sadie's sharp tongue and habit of making pointed remarks about people and situations, she had a soft heart.

By the time Liz was within earshot, the fireman and the chief had forced the door open. Caitlyn insisted Claudia stay seated until the ambulance arrived.

"What happened, Claudia?" the chief asked.

"A dog ran right in front of me," Claudia said. "I had to swerve, and *bam*, the next thing I knew, I hit that tree."

A dog? A terrible feeling tightened in Liz's chest as she scanned the street. Beans, the English bulldog she had inherited with the inn, was the only dog living on this block. But it must have been a stray since she didn't see Beans anywhere. He didn't go far from the inn.

"The air bag saved you," Chief Houghton said to Claudia. "Your injuries would have been much worse without it."

"I know. I feel fine." Claudia attempted to swing one leg out of the vehicle.

"Hold it," Caitlyn said. "Stay right there. Here come the EMTs."

The ambulance raced up, its sirens screaming. The EMTs rushed to join Caitlyn and the chief at the car.

With all the excitement, people had come out of their houses, standing on their porches and in the street, watching.

A small red sports car zoomed up the street from the opposite direction, slowing down at the inn. Then the driver continued toward the crashed vehicle, stopping right in the middle of the street.

A good-looking dark-haired man dressed in a sport coat and jeans jumped out and raced to the vehicle. "Claudia! Claudia, are you all right?" He darted back and forth, trying to get past Chief Houghton.

Finally, the chief took the man's arm and led him off to the side, apparently explaining the situation.

"Who is that?" Liz asked. There were still many people in town she didn't recognize yet.

"That's Claudia's ex," Mary Ann said. "Bob Stevens."

"By his expression, I'd say he still cares," Sadie said drily. "Unusual in an ex-husband."

Sadie appeared to be right, at least about his feelings; Bob was visibly upset. When the EMTs wheeled Claudia toward the ambulance, Bob trotted alongside, trying to get close to her. He even attempted to climb inside the ambulance, but when they rebuffed him, he ran to his car and followed them to the hospital.

Next a tow truck arrived, and the driver began to hook up the wrecked vehicle.

Liz was thinking about heading back to the inn when she glanced across the street and noticed the bushes rustling. A moment later, Beans emerged. Seeing the activity, he stopped short and sniffed the air, his jowls wagging.

"There's your dog." Sadie elbowed Liz. "What's he been up to now?"

"I'm afraid to find out," Liz said. Had he caused the accident? As far as she knew, he didn't usually go over there. To Piper, she said, "I'll be at the inn in five minutes to make you that cup of coffee."

"Don't worry about it," Piper replied. "Tony and I are going over to the Order of the Otter Lodge, where they'll be holding the contest. I'll grab something on the way."

"Are you sure?" Liz felt remiss in her innkeeper duties.

"Absolutely." Piper smiled. "We'll be back for cookie hour."

"You mean coffee hour," Tony said.

"No, cookie hour," Piper shot back.

Still laughing and squabbling, the duo headed down the sidewalk toward the inn.

Liz darted across the street and grabbed Beans by the collar. "You're coming with me, you naughty thing. What were you doing over here?" *And did you run in front of Claudia's car and make her go off the road?*

Beans, of course, didn't answer, but at least he docilely accompanied her across the street.

The tow truck's winch groaned as the chain lifted the car away from the tree, tugging it up onto a flatbed.

Disturbed by the noise, the dog stopped short, all four legs planted.

As the car bumped and thumped into place, Liz noticed something odd. On the ground where it had been was a slick puddle of fluid. She recognized it as brake fluid from previous vehicle problems. The question was—had the leak been caused by the accident, or were Claudia's brakes faulty?

"Did you see that brake fluid?" Sadie asked as she, Mary Ann, and Liz trooped back to the inn, Beans following. Caitlyn had left after seeing off the ambulance.

"I did," Liz said. "I was wondering about it."

"Maybe Claudia's car was tampered with. She tried to brake but slammed right into the tree."

Mary Ann stopped short, hands on her hips. "Sadie Schwarzentruber, who could have possibly tampered with Claudia's car and why?"

Sadie echoed Mary Ann's stance. "I don't know. But tell me this, why would a woman who owns a car dealership be driving around with faulty brakes? Ordinary folks maybe, but her?"

"Ladies, ladies." Liz put up her hands in a conciliatory gesture. "I agree it looked strange, but maybe the leak happened during the accident."

"That's what I think." Mary Ann had a triumphant note in her voice.

"I'm sure they'll investigate," Liz said. "Chief Houghton does a good job."

"I hope so," Sadie said darkly. "The whole thing was very suspicious." She shrugged. "Who crashes a car on this street?"

Only people trying to avoid my dog. Liz smiled wryly at Beans, panting as he trudged along the sidewalk, drool flying off his jowls.

A new Jeep pulled into the inn's drive, and for a moment Liz wondered who it could possibly be. Then she glanced at her watch, realizing with a start it was time for the Greggs to check in. She broke into a trot. "Sorry but I have to go. I've got guests arriving."

Slightly worse for wear, Liz reached the front porch at the same time as her middle-aged guests. "Welcome. I'm your host, Liz Eckardt. Call me Liz."

The man, who had dark curly hair and chiseled features, put his arm around his pretty blonde companion. "Hi, Liz. I'm Ron Gregg, and this is Connie, my wife."

"Come on in." Liz started for the front door only to be halted by Connie's laugh.

"And who is this? Oh, you are darling."

Liz turned to see Connie kneeling beside Beans, who accepted her patting with good grace. "That's Beans. He came with the inn."

The story of the resident bulldog charmed the Greggs, as did the tale of her surprise quilting-shop tenants.

"I'll have to go in there later," Connie said, eyeing the window display. "I love to sew."

Ron gave a good-natured snort. "I'll have to hide the credit cards."

Connie swatted his arm playfully. "Who was the one who bought golf clubs last week?"

"Busted. But they were on sale, remember? End of the season." Ron smiled fondly at Connie, who took his arm and gazed into his eyes.

"Don't mind us," she said. "We've only been married three months."

Liz mentally rearranged the rooms, deciding to put the couple in the Heirloom Room, often used for honeymoons. This must be a second marriage since Connie had mentioned adult children when booking.

"When is the rest of your party arriving?" Liz led them to the reception desk.

To her shock, Connie's mood shifted abruptly from blissful happiness to outright distress. Her eyes were tearful as she said, "You tell her, Ron." She turned and buried her head in Ron's chest. He put his arm around her and patted her back.

"As Connie mentioned, we've only been married three months." His jaw worked for a moment. Then he continued. "Our children weren't exactly happy about it, although both of us have been divorced for ages. We planned this getaway so everyone could get to know each other and hopefully bond as a family."

"That sounds nice," Liz said. It must be difficult for stepfamilies to build relationships when the children were already adults.

"We thought it would be. Connie's daughter Brooke said she'd help convince the others." Ron shook his head. "But now she told us she's not sure she'll be able to be here. Same with her sister, Taylor."

"And we haven't heard anything at all from Ron's two, Jake and Jessica," Connie said with a sniff.

"I'm so sorry to hear that. Do you want me to hold the rooms anyway?" Liz sent up a quick prayer that this family rift would be mended soon, preferably before Thanksgiving.

The couple exchanged glances.

"Would you?" Ron asked. "I'll pay for them, of course."

Connie beamed at her husband. "You are wonderful. I hope those kids appreciate how wonderful."

Liz couldn't argue with his proposition, although the size of the needed turkey took a nosedive with the loss of four guests. Maybe she should cook Cornish hens instead.

After signing them in and noting they were from Blaketown, a nearby city, she gave them a flyer detailing the events scheduled for A Pleasant Creek Thanksgiving. "I don't know if you heard about it, but there's a lot going on in town this week. Maybe you'll see something you want to do."

Connie crowed as she jabbed a finger at one listing. "The pie contest. I'm already entered. Nationals, here I come."

"Connie's a great baker," Ron said. "She's won many ribbons for her pies."

Liz felt a pang of competitiveness on behalf of her friend. "Really? I know someone who wins prizes too. Mary Ann Berne."

"I know her," Connie said. "We duke it out at the county fair every year, remember, Ron?"

Uh-oh. Mary Ann had a serious rival staying right here under Liz's roof. "I should warn you," Liz said. "She's in the contest too."

"Good. The more the merrier." Connie leaned forward across the counter. "One more thing. May I use your kitchen to make my pies?"

How could Liz refuse? The couple was spending thousands for a nine-day booking. She glanced at the shop entrance. But how would Mary Ann react to Liz supporting one of her rivals, even if indirectly?

Liz swallowed hard. "Of course you can. And may the best pie win." She grabbed the keys to the Heirloom Room. "Let me show you to your room."

Connie adored the Heirloom Room, as did most women who set eyes on it. She oohed and aahed over the enormous four-poster bed with its light blue canopy, the white carved fireplace, the Tiffany lamps, the antique chest, and the comfortable contemporary sofa. She and Ron both loved the hot tub in the huge bathroom.

With a final word about coffee hour, Liz left them alone and headed downstairs.

Sarah Borkholder, her part-time employee, was in the kitchen pulling cookie supplies out of the cupboards. She was almost family, since she had married Isaac, the son of Liz's cousin and good friend Miriam Borkholder.

"I didn't even see you arrive." Liz went to the coffeemaker to brew a pot.

"I got here while you were all down at the accident," Sarah said in her soft voice. She wore the traditional Amish garb of a dark blue dress covered by a white apron. A black *Kapp* sat atop her blonde head. "I cleaned the two bedrooms that needed it, then came down here."

"You are so efficient. I don't know what I'd do without you." Liz was speaking the truth. Sarah always seemed to know what needed doing and did it without complaint.

"Thank you. I appreciate that." Sarah measured out a cup of raisins and dumped them into a pot. She added water and set it on the stove.

"What are you making?" Liz asked. She removed two mugs from the cupboard.

"Raisin cookies. They are very tasty. You will see."

Liz poured coffee and sipped while watching Sarah put together the cookies. After boiling the raisins down, she added them and some of the liquid to a mixture of creamed butter, egg, vanilla, and dry ingredients.

"Are you looking forward to Thanksgiving?" Liz asked. Although the Amish were restrained when celebrating holidays, they enjoyed Thanksgiving and Christmas.

"I am." Sarah smiled. "I plan to make my husband some delicious traditional dishes."

"He's a lucky man."

"I hope you can join us on Thanksgiving," Sarah said. "We would love to have you as our guest."

Liz was touched. "That is so kind of you. But I'll be serving dinner here for my guests, so I don't think I can."

"Keep it in mind anyway. Maybe something will work out." Sarah slid a tray of cookies into the oven and poured herself a cup of coffee. She joined Liz at the table. "On another topic, was that woman all right? The one who was in the accident today?"

"I think so. It was Claudia Stevens. She owns the auto dealership with the same name."

"Oh yes. I have heard of her, though of course we do not patronize her business." Sarah's tone was wry. Like all traditional Amish, Sarah and her family used a horse and buggy.

"I think Beans might have caused the accident." Liz lowered her voice, although there was no way the dog could hear her from his favorite spot sleeping by the front door.

Sarah appeared stunned. "Beans? That is not possible. Did she say she saw him?"

"Not specifically. She said a dog ran in front of her."

The young woman's lips quirked. "Beans? Run? Those two words don't go together."

Liz laughed, relieved. "You're right. It must have been another dog." She glanced at the clock. "It's almost coffee hour."

As if on cue, the front door opened, and Liz heard voices, one male, one female. Tony and Piper must be back. She pushed away from the table and stood. "I'll start a fresh pot of coffee."

Sarah jumped up. "And I will finish the cookies." She hurried to pull out the pans of cookies.

By the time Piper and Tony returned from freshening up, Connie and Ron had come downstairs for coffee hour. Liz noticed the foursome was busy chatting away. She loved this aspect of running an inn, bringing people together to create new friendships. Many of her guests would never have met otherwise.

The cookies were a hit, and Liz enjoyed the crunchy yet chewy treat too.

While Liz was in the kitchen fetching more cookies, Connie popped in. She gazed around, admiring the spacious room. "I wanted to double-check with you that it's really okay for me to bake my pies in here."

"Certainly. Make yourself at home." Liz opened a couple of cabinet doors to show Connie where the baking supplies were located. "I'm assuming you'll pick up your own ingredients?"

"Of course I will." Connie had the grace to blush. "I know I was presuming a lot, that you would let me use your kitchen. But we'd already booked the trip when I found out about the contest, and it seemed like something I couldn't pass up."

"Say no more." Liz removed the brewed pot from the coffeemaker.

"Thank you so much." Connie gave Liz an impulsive and thankfully brief hug. "I'm so excited the Baking Bonanza is going to be on television."

"It is wonderful news," Liz said. "It will bring a good deal of attention to Pleasant Creek too, which is nice."

After Connie darted out of the kitchen, Sarah entered, her face downcast.

"Is something wrong?" Liz asked. Sarah was almost never gloomy.

The young woman looked up, startled. "I am sorry. I was lost in thought." By the look on her face, Liz knew there was more.

"What is it?" Liz asked gently.

Sarah shifted from foot to foot, but finally she said, "The television woman—Piper Reynolds—was asking me questions."

Liz felt a twinge of concern. "What kind of questions?"

"About my family, mostly. And about other Amish people in the area."

That sounded innocuous enough. "I'm sure she's only interested and curious, like many visitors."

"You are probably right." But by the doubt on Sarah's face, Liz knew she didn't really believe that.

Did Piper Reynolds have another reason besides the pie contest to come to Pleasant Creek?

3

The thump of a bass drum followed by a shrill blat of trumpets announced the Thanksgiving parade was on its way. The crowd around Liz, standing near the clock tower in the town square, buzzed with anticipation. Children rode on their fathers' shoulders, mothers rocked strollers, couples stood arm in arm. Even Liz felt a thrill of excitement participating in this heartwarming small-town event.

Sadie pushed through the throng. "Liz, you made it." She carried a corn dog, a favorite at most Indiana festivals and fairs.

"I wouldn't miss it for anything." Liz glanced around. "Everyone in town must be here."

"Almost." Sadie scanned the crowd. "A lot of visitors too, I'm guessing. Of course we've got the football game later, and people are here for that."

"Football game?" Liz knew that Hoosiers went wild over basketball, but she didn't know much about local football.

"Tonight is the big game between Pleasant Creek and Blaketown. They're our biggest rivals." Sadie nudged Liz. "Here we go."

First down the street were two men carrying a huge banner reading, "Welcome to A Pleasant Creek Thanksgiving." The high school brass band followed, the teens marching in rhythm, swinging their instruments between musical selections.

Tony, camera to his eye, tracked the parade, turning now and then to record the reactions of the audience.

Next came a group of young schoolchildren dressed as turkeys and Pilgrims. In front of where Liz and Sadie stood, they paused to do a routine similar to a square dance.

"Aren't they cute?" Sadie's eyes were suspiciously bright. "I remember when my grandson used to be a turkey in school Thanksgiving celebrations."

"I have those fond memories too." Steve, whom Liz had raised from the age of seven after her good friends died in a car accident, had been a Cub Scout and in the school band. As a result, Liz had attended many parades and events similar to this one.

One little boy lost his turkey headpiece in a gust of wind, and a stray dog snatched it up and ran off with it. The spectators hooted and laughed. Someone in the crowd managed to recover the headpiece, slightly rumpled but still usable, and the boy put it back on. The children continued marching in an uneven formation.

"Only in Pleasant Creek." Sadie shook her head. "That reminds me. You might know this already, but if you need to buy a turkey, go out to the Mast farm. They have the best." She curled her lips. "You won't ever eat a frozen supermarket turkey again."

"Mast. Thanks. I'll check it out." Liz welcomed the suggestion since she wanted to make this year's meal extra special.

Next was a float from the hardware store, featuring a live display of Pilgrims cooking over a fake fire. Tools from the store were scattered throughout the display, including a chain saw.

"I'll bet the Pilgrims wished they had one of those chain saws," Sadie said. "I can't imagine clearing trees by hand."

Liz's gaze was caught by a bright blue classic convertible trundling down the street. Thanks to the car buffs in her life, she recognized it as a 1956 Chevrolet Bel Air. "Isn't that Jackson sitting in the backseat?"

The mayor sat stiffly upright, waving at the crowd on both sides of the street.

Sadie squinted. "Sure is. Right next to Claudia Stevens. She must be fully recovered from her accident since she's out this evening. That's good news."

Liz studied Jackson's companion. In contrast to Jackson, Claudia seemed to enjoy having an audience. She beamed ear to ear as people called out greetings, one young man even running alongside the slow-moving car to give her a high five.

A middle-aged woman wearing a Pleasant Creek sweatshirt turned to Sadie, her eyes wide. "Did you hear? Claudia is going to run for mayor next year against Jackson. Boy, will that be a hard choice. Jackson's great, but Claudia has lots of good ideas. And she promised to lower taxes."

Don't they all? Liz's loyalty to Jackson wasn't swayed an inch.

Sadie nodded sagely. "I told you she wasn't Jackson's best friend."

As the convertible passed in front of them, Liz waved and hopped up and down, trying to attract the mayor's attention. "Jackson! Jackson!"

She was rewarded with the mayor's huge, genuine smile.

Claudia turned to see who he was grinning at. For good measure, Liz waved at her too, and the businesswoman gave her a limp flutter of her fingertips in reply.

"You should manage his campaign," Sadie suggested. "You're obviously his biggest fan."

Liz's cheeks heated up. "I was only being supportive." She quickly changed the subject. "Look at the cheerleaders. They're awesome, like gymnasts."

A group of girls and several guys executed flips, handstands, and formations while shouting out cheers for the Pleasant Creek football team.

"Believe it or not, but I used to be a gymnast in high school," Sadie said. "I was one of the best."

"I believe it," Liz said, picturing the energetic Sadie performing for a crowd.

After the parade, everyone made a mass exodus to the high school to watch the football game. Liz was walking toward the bleachers when she heard her name being called. With a lift of her spirits, she turned to see Jackson jogging toward her.

"I hoped you'd be here tonight," he said.

"I wouldn't miss it." She rearranged the lap blanket she held and shifted the tote containing a thermos of hot chocolate to a more comfortable position on her arm.

"I see you brought supplies." Jackson fell into step beside her. "How about I buy us a couple of hot dogs and fries? They're good here."

"That sounds great." On a crisp night like this, the greasy treats sounded like they'd hit the spot. "I like relish, mustard, and ketchup on my hot dogs." Liz pointed to her bag. "I brought an extra cup for hot chocolate, so you're welcome to have some."

He gave her a thumbs-up. "Get us a seat and I'll find you." He jogged off again.

Liz found a spot several rows up, a good location to watch the game as well as the spectators, many mingling on the edge of the field. Games were obviously a social event, a time for friends and neighbors to greet each other and catch up.

After a few minutes, Jackson headed toward her, carrying a cardboard tray. He settled beside her, mouthwatering aromas drifting her way. "Put out your hand."

She complied, and he set a hot dog and bun resting in a little tray in her hand. She smiled. "The condiments look just right."

"I'm glad." Jackson took a big bite of his own hot dog and chewed.

Liz nibbled at hers, the blend of savory and spicy flavors bursting in her mouth. "Yum."

"Try a fry." He held out a container crammed with crispy french fries.

These, too, were perfectly cooked and tasty. "There's something about eating outdoors that makes everything taste better."

"I agree." Jackson took the last couple of bites of his hot dog and wiped his fingers on a napkin. "Here comes the kickoff."

The away team won the coin toss and kicked the ball to start the game. The players began to grapple and run.

"Are you a football fan?" Jackson asked.

Liz hedged for a moment, then decided to be honest. "Not really."

He pulled his head back, giving her a mock look of horror. "Tell me it isn't so."

She laughed at his expression. "I'm sorry. My ex-boyfriend was a huge fan, and I think he explained the rules of the game to me every time we watched together. But by the next game, I'd forget everything."

Jackson sighed. "Oh, well. Just make sure you root for Pleasant Creek."

"Of course I will." Liz reached for another crispy fry and dipped it in a pool of ketchup. Then she pulled out the thermos and poured them each a cup of cocoa.

Jackson blew on his and took a sip. "This is good. Thanks."

As the teams ran back and forth down the field, their actions punctuated with whistles from the referees, Liz soaked in the atmosphere and relaxed. She saw Mary Ann and Sadie arrive, and she spotted the Greggs seated a few rows down with Bob Stevens, Claudia's ex-husband. How did they know him?

Piper and Tony had arrived, and they were walking around filming snippets of the action on the field and in the stands.

Liz elbowed Jackson, then pointed at her guests. "We've got a television crew in town filming. Not actually a 'crew,' I guess. There are just two of them. They're staying at the inn."

Jackson followed her finger. "Oh yeah, I saw those two at the parade. What are they doing here?"

Liz was pleased to be the first to share the exciting news with Jackson. "You haven't heard? The pie Baking Bonanza is going to be on national television. Piper has a food show called *Taste and Tour*."

"That's great news for the town. And the contestants." He took another sip of cocoa. "I've seen an episode or two of the show. I liked the Memphis ribs segment. I used one of the dry-rub recipes last summer."

Liz resolved to find past episodes to watch. She was apparently one of the few people in Pleasant Creek who hadn't seen the show.

Jackson cheered at something that happened on the field. "We're on our way to a touchdown."

"Wonderful." Liz smiled.

On the edge of the field, Claudia strolled by with a male companion, a tall, lanky man with a long face and buck teeth.

Jackson groaned and ducked his head as Claudia's piercing gaze roamed the crowd on the bleachers. "Sorry. It's just that I've had my fill of Claudia today."

Liz hadn't planned to bring up the subject, but now that he had, she felt free to comment. "You didn't look very happy in that convertible. I thought maybe you didn't like being on display."

"I don't really, but I can handle it." Jackson shook his head and sighed. "I used to be friends with Claudia and her ex-husband, Bob—until she decided to run for office against me." He pressed his lips together. "Rivalry brings out the worst in some people."

"That's what Sadie implied earlier. We don't have to talk about it if you don't want to."

"I don't mind. It feels good to get it off my chest." He rubbed his chin, thinking. "I ran for mayor because I wanted to do something good for my hometown. Being a business owner gives me a unique perspective on how the town can attract new companies as well as visitors."

"You've got my vote." Liz opened the thermos and topped off their cups. "I definitely want to see more tourists in town. That's how I make my living."

"You and most of the chamber members feel that way. That's why I was blindsided when Claudia ran a . . . shall we say, less-than-kind campaign."

"That's too bad." Liz meant it. In her work as an attorney she'd seen her share of controversy, acrimony, and contentious relationships. Although being an innkeeper wasn't always blissful, she didn't miss the adversarial side of practicing law.

"It is. I'm not looking forward to the next race. In fact, I may step down."

Liz studied Jackson's gloomy expression with concern. He was defeated before he even tried. "Don't say that. The town needs you."

"You're the best. Thanks." Jackson's face lightened. Then he handed his cocoa to Liz, jumped up, and yelled, "Go, Pleasant Creek! That's it, run, run, run!" He punched his fist in the air. "You've got it!" He beamed down at Liz. "Touchdown!"

All around them, people leaped up to cheer and shout, ecstatic about the game's first score. Through the standing bodies, Liz saw the Greggs were still seated, although Bob had gotten to his feet with the rest of the Pleasant Creek fans. His attention was only half on the game, Liz noticed, because he turned to stare at Claudia, sitting at the other end with her male companion.

"Who's that with Claudia?" Liz asked when Jackson sat down.

He craned his neck to look, then waved when Claudia spotted

him. "That's Kevin Fiske, her business partner. She brought him in after the divorce."

"That was kind of an unusual settlement, wasn't it? A wife getting the family business."

Jackson's smile was wry. "That's Claudia for you. She always comes out ahead."

"Not always, Mr. Mayor."

A short while later, Liz decided she needed to visit the facilities. Jackson directed her to the school locker rooms, a distance away across the field. It took a few minutes to inch down the bleachers without tripping over someone or knocking over their drinks. Finally, she reached the grass and started the trek to the building, passing other people coming her way.

The door to the section marked Girls was propped open, and Liz stepped inside. This was the locker room proper, with bathroom stalls and showers in another room. As she walked past a row of lockers, she heard a woman's voice raised in anger. "You know the right thing to do. And you'd better do it."

Liz paused, alarmed at the woman's words and tone of voice. Was she stepping into an argument? Maybe she should retreat, but she really needed . . .

"Don't you threaten me," another woman said. Her laugh was nasty. "It didn't work then, and it won't work now."

Oh, my. Liz turned on her heel to leave as footsteps clattered on the tile. Too late.

A woman appeared in the doorway to the stalls, moving fast, fists clenched at her sides. It was Claudia.

4

"**M**s. Stevens?" Liz asked, realizing they hadn't been introduced. "I'm Liz Eckardt, owner of the Olde Mansion Inn."

Claudia paused, just barely, on her toes as though hoping to fly away. "Oh yes. Nice to meet you."

"I was on the scene of your accident this afternoon. I'm glad to see that you're all right."

The business owner touched her head. "Just a scratch on my forehead. The air bag saved me. Well, Ms. Eckardt . . ." She turned to leave.

"Do you know what happened? I heard you say a dog ran in front of you." Liz's heart clenched at the idea that Beans might have caused her accident.

Claudia waved a hand with a laugh. "Oh, one did. But it was all my fault. I was going too fast, and I couldn't stop in time."

"What did the dog look like?" She held her breath for the answer.

"I don't remember. It was all a blur, I'm afraid." She stepped toward the doorway.

Maybe Beans was innocent after all. "So there wasn't something wrong with the brakes? I saw fluid—"

"Of course there wasn't anything wrong with the brakes." Claudia drew back, affronted. "I get my car serviced at my own garage, and I assure you, we do top-notch work."

"I'm sure you do. I didn't—" Liz sighed as Claudia marched out of the locker room, the set of her head and shoulders conveying annoyance. Liz had put her foot in her mouth for sure. Remembering why she was even in the locker room to begin with, she hurried toward the bathroom.

Connie Greggs stood at a sink washing her hands. She glanced over in surprise. "Hi, Liz. I didn't know you were at the game."

"I'm sitting above you in the bleachers." No one else was in the restroom, so that meant Claudia had been arguing with Connie. *About what?* To hide her confusion, Liz said, "Too bad for Blaketown about the Pleasant Creek touchdown."

"The game's not over yet." Connie pushed the paper towel lever a few times. "Actually, I grew up in Pleasant Creek. My husband is the Blaketown fan."

"Really? That must be fun, supporting opposite teams."

"It keeps things interesting. See you later."

When Liz rejoined Jackson in the stands, she resolutely put aside her questions and concerns about Claudia's accident. She also shelved the apparent conflict between her guest and the dealership owner. It wasn't any of her business, although she wondered about animosities that survived decades of adult life after Connie had left town. Memories were long in small towns; she'd learned that while living in Pleasant Creek.

Rivalries were also long-standing, and the game was a close one that teased and tormented both sides. Finally, Pleasant Creek won 21 to 17 to the jubilation of local fans and promises of a comeback by the other side.

"It was nice watching the game with you," Jackson said as he escorted Liz to her car. His eyes twinkled. "Even if you didn't understand what was going on."

"Our team won, and that's all I need to know." Liz unlocked the car door. "Are you going to the craft fair in the square tomorrow?" She was looking forward to selecting Christmas presents from among the handmade items.

"Definitely. See you there." Jackson waited until Liz was inside her car and had the motor started, and then with a wave, he headed off to his own vehicle.

His manners really were impeccable, Liz realized with pleasure. He was a great companion too. *Maybe I'll bone up on the rules of football. Won't that surprise Jackson?*

Despite the slow traffic leaving the field, Liz arrived back at the inn before her guests. After lighting a fire in the fireplace, she turned on a few more lights and then filled a kettle, planning to offer them hot drinks before bedtime.

The front door opened, and she heard footsteps in the hall and the voices of Connie and Ron. She hurried out to greet them. "I just put the kettle on for tea or decaf coffee," she said. "Would you like a cup?"

"That sounds perfect," Connie said, unbuttoning her coat. "This place looked so cozy when we drove up, as if all the lights in the windows were beckoning us home."

Ron took his wife's coat and hung it up. "It certainly did."

"I'm so glad." Liz's heart warmed. That was her goal, to create a comforting and welcoming ambience for her guests. "Make yourselves comfortable in the sitting room, and I'll be right in." She led the way to the elegant yet cozy room with stained glass windows, a marble fireplace, and cushy furnishings.

As Liz put together a tray with hot water, mugs, a selection of drink choices, and a plate of cookies, she heard the front door open again. By the time she joined her guests, Piper was seated there with the Greggs. The television star looked tired, slouched in an armchair with her feet up on a hassock. In contrast, the newlyweds cuddled close on the sofa, bright-eyed and smiling.

"Hi, Piper." Liz set the tray on the coffee table. "You can have my cup, and I'll go get another."

Piper turned her head slowly. "Thanks." She yawned, covering her mouth with one hand. "I'm sorry. I shouldn't be this exhausted. It's still early on the West Coast."

"It must be hard getting used to the time changes." Connie leaned forward and selected tea bags for herself and her husband. "Zipping back and forth from coast to coast would be enough to make your head spin."

Piper gave a little laugh. "True. My body clock is always out of whack."

"Is Tony still out?" Liz offered the tea basket to Piper, who leafed through and chose chamomile. "Good choice. That herb will help you get a good night's rest."

"He went to hear a local band play," Piper said. "Some guys he met told him about it."

"That's why I give out keys. Guests can come and go as they please." Liz poured hot water for everyone, then darted back to the kitchen for a mug. She, too, chose a relaxing herbal blend, hoping to get a good night's sleep.

"How is it being back in your hometown?" Liz asked Connie to make conversation. Then she bit her tongue, remembering Connie's squabble with Claudia.

"It's okay," Connie said. "I ran into a few people I used to know."

"I'll say." Ron gave his wife a teasing smile. "Wasn't that one of your old boyfriends we were sitting with?"

"Bob? That's ancient history." Connie tapped him on the nose. "Nothing to be jealous about there."

He playfully snapped his teeth at her finger, and they both laughed.

Liz and Piper exchanged glances, the other woman giving a discreet eye roll. Liz appreciated couples in love, but in this case, Connie and Ron were a little too saccharine for her taste.

"Oh, so you know Bob Stevens?" Liz asked, again, more to say something than because she really cared.

"And his ex." Connie made a face. "Claudia's still as stuck-up and selfish as she was in high school."

"Now, now," Ron said. "Don't be unkind."

Connie's face reddened. "Is it unkind if it's true? Look what she did to Bob. He's practically penniless."

Ron shrugged, looking uncomfortable. "He's not a good businessman. I'm sure glad I didn't invest in that last venture of his. It's already belly-up."

"Well, if Claudia wasn't so greedy—" Connie seemed to remember where she was. "I'm sorry, Liz, Piper. I didn't expect to have such a strong reaction to my hometown and people I used to know."

"I hear you," Piper muttered.

Liz wondered where Piper had grown up. By the look on her face, it hadn't been a happy experience.

"Connie hasn't been back here for years," Ron said. "She lived in Indianapolis for what—twenty years, hon?"

"Twenty-five. Moved there right after I got married." A look of pain crossed Connie's face. "Then I got divorced . . ."

Ron put his arm around her. "It wasn't your fault. Don't forget that."

"No, he left me." Connie shifted to face him. "And in your case, she dropped you, and I picked you up."

He leaned close, nose to nose. "I'm sure glad you did."

They were back to billing and cooing. Liz felt like her head was spinning from the emotional roller coaster that was the Connie and

Ron show. She glanced at Piper, who had a greenish cast to her face. Was she ill, or was she suffering from an overdose of vicarious romance?

Piper slid out of the chair and stood, setting down her mug on the side table. "I'm going upstairs. I can't keep my eyes open."

"Sleep well," Liz said. "I put coffee on at seven, and breakfast is whenever you want it."

"Thanks, Liz. Good night, Connie, Ron." Piper headed for the doorway.

"Hold on, Piper," Connie said. "For a minute there, you reminded me of someone I used to know. One of my younger sister's friends." She squinted. "You didn't grow up around here, did you?"

Piper laughed. "I get that all the time, people coming up to me and telling me I look familiar. It's because they see me on television." She waved. "See you in the morning."

After Piper climbed the stairs, Connie said, "I still think she's the spitting image of that girl . . . What was her name?"

"I have no idea." Ron drained his tea. "But I doubt they're related. Doesn't Piper come from California?"

"Just because you're on TV doesn't mean you were born in California," Connie said. "David Letterman grew up in Indianapolis."

"I didn't know that," Liz said. She also drank the last of her tea, hoping the Greggs would decide to retire soon too. Although she could certainly go to bed while guests were still awake, she liked to check the windows and doors, and make sure everything—and everyone—was tucked in for the night. Then she remembered Tony was still out. Well, almost everyone then.

"Liz, the pie contest is on Monday so I'll bake on Sunday," Connie said. "Is that okay with you?"

"That sounds fine. You can use the kitchen midafternoon or after dinner, whatever works."

"Do you need a taste tester?" Ron waved a hand. "I'll volunteer."

Connie tapped her lips with one finger, pretending to consider his offer. "I don't think so. But maybe I'll bake an extra pie or two. How's that?"

"Awesome." Ron turned to Liz. "She's going to win this thing."

Connie squealed and shoved his shoulder. "Don't jinx me." She glanced at Liz. "Besides, Liz is rooting for her friend."

"I am, but I'll also root for you." What else could Liz say?

Showing unexpected sensitivity, Ron said, "Why don't we head upstairs and let Liz have a few minutes to herself?"

"Stay up as long as you want," Liz felt compelled to say.

Ron levered himself to his feet with a groan, then held out his hand for his wife to grab. "No, no. We've taken up enough of your evening."

Connie didn't protest, and a few minutes later, after extended thank-yous and good nights, Liz was finally alone. Well, almost. Beans lumbered in from his resting place in the hall and lay down in front of the fire with a sigh.

Liz laughed. "That's exactly how I feel, buddy. I love people . . . but I sure love time alone too."

After tidying up the tea things, Liz banked the fire and checked that everything was buttoned up for the night. Then she retired to her quarters, located off the kitchen. The tablet computer on the table in her little sitting room called to her, and before she knew it, she was engrossed in old episodes of Piper's show.

The young woman had a lively, engaging style that came across well on the screen. The people she interviewed seemed to feel real affection for her, developed during the process of Piper learning about what they were cooking, the history of the food, and the special features of that part of the country.

Liz especially enjoyed a segment on baked beans, filmed partially in her old hometown, Boston, as well as in Maine. Boston cream pie made an appearance too, and after seeing how easy it was to make the custard-filled cake treat, Liz decided to give it a try sometime. The website handily included recipes, and she sent a few to the printer.

The site also featured a biography of Piper, who had gone to film school at the University of California. Cooking shows appeared to be her niche, since she'd worked as an assistant on several before being offered her own show.

There was no mention of her parents or life prior to Hollywood, Liz noticed. She checked a couple of other biographies on the same channel to see what was standard and found that they all included place of birth and parent names and occupations.

How strange. Why had Piper omitted that seemingly innocuous information? It was like she didn't exist before her college days.

In a burst of compunction, Liz closed the browser. It wasn't any of her business if Piper had a childhood she chose to forget. Maybe she'd even changed her name. Didn't many show business people do that? She really should put away the attorney mind-set that made her dig into situations that didn't feel or look right. Although, doing so had solved several cases here in Pleasant Creek—

Rap! Rap! Rap!

Liz jumped, her behind literally hopping off the chair. The sound came again, and this time she located its source—it was at the window.

Hands shaking in shock, she crossed the room and pulled open the curtains.

A man's face, hideously marked, stared in at her.

5

Liz screamed and backed away from the window. Where was her cell? She glanced over her shoulder. There it was on the table—

Her name being shouted penetrated her fog of panic. "Liz! Liz, it's me, Tony."

Blinking, she took another look at the man in the window, and the monstrous visage dissolved into the handsome young man's face—sporting a huge black eye. Liz shook her head with a laugh and gestured for him to go around to the back door.

"You almost scared the life out of me," Liz said when she opened the door for Tony. "I thought you had a key."

The cameraman looked sheepish. "I'm sorry. I accidently left my key up in my room. I was going to call Piper to come down and let me in when I saw the light in your window."

Liz studied his black eye under the glare of the kitchen light. "That looks like it hurts. Do you want ice?"

He touched the injured area with tentative fingers. "Thanks. I think I will take some. It's starting to throb."

"Have a seat." Liz opened the freezer and bundled some ice cubes into a clean dish towel. She handed the package to Tony, who held it to his face. "How about ibuprofen or aspirin?" She found both in one of the cabinets. "That will help the pain and inflammation."

"Ibuprofen would be great." Tony grinned at her. "You really do take good care of your guests. Even those who scare you."

"I try. There's never a dull moment around here, believe me." Liz set the medicine bottle and a glass of water on the table. "How about a hot drink? I've got some herbal tea that will help you sleep."

"Yeah, I'll take a cup. My grandmother always makes me tea when I'm home in Chicago."

"You'll get to see her at Thanksgiving?" Liz filled the kettle and placed it on the stove. She got down two mugs from the cabinet, deciding she'd have another cup.

"I sure will. The whole gang will be getting together at my parents' house. Four generations under one roof now that my sister has a kid." He flipped through the tea bags in the basket Liz put in front of him. "Baby Tony, named after me."

"That sounds wonderful." To forestall the obvious questions about her own family, Liz mentioned Steve, then said, "I was happy to discover long-lost Amish relatives when I moved to Pleasant Creek."

"Seriously? That's awesome." Tony's good eye widened in pleasure.

Liz poured hot water into the mugs and settled at the table. "It is indeed." She gave him an overview of her mother's story and her quest to connect with her mother's family.

"The Amish are fascinating," Tony said. "They have this whole separate culture existing in tandem with typical American life." He thought for a moment. "Kind of like Chinatown in Chicago."

"Almost all immigrants have enclaves," Liz said. "But in the case of the Amish, they're maintaining the lifestyle and values of over a hundred years ago. Many people find that intriguing."

Tony laughed. "Yeah, no cars, no TVs, no computers . . . all the things that make modern life so much fun. Or annoying—take your pick."

Liz finally broached the question burning in her mind. "So, what happened tonight? How did you get that shiner?"

Tony grimaced. "I got into a brawl at a nightclub." He quickly raised a hand. "But I didn't start it. Two guys nearby starting swinging at each other, and before I knew it, everyone around them was throwing punches. Some guy jumped me, so I had to fight back. The police had to come break it up."

"Did anyone get arrested?"

"Nope. Chief Houghton answered the call. He gave everyone a warning and let us go." Tony shrugged. "I think he knew the instigators, these two older dudes. Bob and Kevin, I heard him say."

Bob Stevens and Kevin Fiske? Those two names came immediately to Liz's mind.

Before she could ask for more details, Tony said, "One of them—Bob, I think—came to that accident today. I remember seeing him drive up in a red sports car."

"Yes, that's Bob Stevens. I wonder what they were fighting about." *Claudia or the business? Or both?*

"I'm not sure, but Bob threatened to kill Kevin right before Kevin decked him." Tony chuckled. "Big drama in a small town."

"Isn't that always the way?" Liz pondered Tony's revelation, fitting the information into the little she knew.

Tony took a deep, audible breath. "Is your friend Caitlyn single?"

Liz studied his hopeful expression with amusement. "Why, yes, she is. Are you interested in asking her out?"

"I am. Not only is she cute, but the way she handled that car accident . . . Wow." He shook his head. "She's a good person to know in an emergency."

"Yes, she certainly is. Too bad she isn't here right now." Liz gestured at his black eye.

"I'm glad she isn't." Tony flushed, red creeping up his neck. "Talk about embarrassing. I've got to go around town sporting a black eye. It's not exactly attractive."

"Maybe Piper can put makeup on it," Liz said mischievously.

To her surprise, Tony snapped his fingers and said, "Good point. She's got some heavy-duty stuff in her makeup bag." He glanced at the clock on the stove. "Yikes. I'd better get to bed. Piper wants to start early in the morning."

"Me too." Liz gathered the mugs. "I'm really glad you two are here. Your show will be a big boost for the town."

"I'm glad you feel that way. Piper had to work hard to get the segment. The producers wanted her to go to Plymouth, Massachusetts, and film their Thanksgiving festival. But she fought for Pleasant Creek and won." Tony smiled. "She made a good point. Everyone covers that event. We try to be different."

"How did she even hear about the Pleasant Creek event? This is the first year we've held it."

"I'm not sure. Someone told her about it, maybe." He patted his pockets. "Good. I do have the room key. See you in the morning."

Liz performed the last little chores before bed, half her mind on the conversation with Tony. Hostilities between Bob and Kevin, the man who replaced him at the dealership, were certainly intense if death threats were made. Both men seemed educated and civilized, not the type to engage in barroom brawls. Was Kevin involved with Claudia? Even more than money, love sparked trouble.

As for Piper, it was to the town's benefit that she had chosen to cover the pie Baking Bonanza rather than a larger, more well-known event. But Liz wondered if there was a personal motive behind her choice.

———————

"Good morning, Miss Eckardt." Sarah Borkholder entered the kitchen. "How are you today?"

Liz looked up from the oven, where she was sliding a pan of popovers in to bake. "I'm doing well. How are you?"

"I am fine, thanks." Sarah slipped off her coat and smiled. "Everyone at home is excited, getting ready for the holiday next week."

"It's a wonderful time of year," Liz said, removing a carton of eggs from the fridge. "Can you please slice the melon for me?" At Sarah's nod, she opened the crisper drawer and grabbed a cantaloupe.

Sarah retrieved a cutting board and a knife and got to work on the fruit while Liz dug out her favorite striped mixing bowl. Scrambled eggs, popovers, and link sausage were on the menu this morning with melon and an assortment of jams.

Piper appeared in the doorway, staring at the cell phone in her hand.

"Coffee's on," Liz said. "Help yourself."

The television star glanced up. "Oh, great. Thanks." She waved the phone. "I forgot to plug this in last night. Do you believe it's totally dead? And of course I'm expecting a call."

"There are outlets in the sitting room. Feel free to have a seat in there while we finish making breakfast."

As Piper poured a cup of coffee, she sniffed appreciatively. "I'm starving. It must be all the fresh air."

"That will do it." Liz poured beaten eggs into a hot pan. On the back burner, sausages popped and sizzled.

Piper poured a cup of coffee, then added milk and sugar. Liz noticed that she kept glancing at Sarah, who looked neat and trim in her gray dress, apron, and Kapp. She hoped Piper wasn't thinking about trying to interview any Amish as part of the show. Their beliefs prohibited being filmed or photographed, and even just asking them to participate might be seen as offensive. Liz decided to keep an eye on the situation and step in if need be.

Cradling her cup of coffee and her phone, Piper headed out of the room.

The Greggs bounded downstairs next, and they eagerly sat down to eat when Liz and Sarah set out the platters of food. Piper joined them soon after. Liz allowed the guests to help themselves, family-style, while she filled coffee mugs and juice glasses.

"I adore popovers. And is this homemade strawberry jam?" Connie asked as she spread ruby-red preserves on her pastry.

"It is indeed," Liz said. "I bought it at the farmers' market last summer."

Finished with kitchen chores, Sarah went upstairs and got started on making beds and cleaning the bathrooms.

"Aren't we missing someone?" Ron glanced around.

"Tony," Piper said. "He'll be down in a minute."

As if conjured by her words, they heard whistling on the stairs, and a moment later the smiling cameraman popped into the room. He looked crisp and fresh in a white shirt and jeans, and in the clear morning light, his black eye sported lovely shades of purple and burgundy.

Connie yelped, dropping the jam serving spoon and sending a glob of red onto the cloth. "What happened to you?"

"You should see the other guy." Tony gave a cheeky grin and slid into a chair beside Piper. He flicked open his napkin. "Would you please pass me the eggs?"

As the group ate, Tony filled them in on the events of the night before, fortunately not bothering to share the names of participants, Liz noticed. She could just imagine Connie's reaction to learning her former boyfriend had been brawling in a public place.

Since her guests were satisfied for the moment, Liz went into the main sitting room to tidy up. She swept the old ashes out of the fireplace and laid a fire, ready for her to light that afternoon. Piper had left her used mug on an end table, and as Liz picked it up, she noticed a piece of paper covered with doodles next to it. Among the flowers and squares was the name *Elmo*, outlined heavily in ink.

Elmo was an old-fashioned name, used most often these days by the Amish, or by the makers of a children's toy, Liz realized with a smile. She crumpled the piece of paper and tossed it into the trash, wondering once again exactly why Piper had come to Pleasant Creek.

Sarah helped her clear the breakfast dishes, and after the dishwasher was humming, Liz took a detour into Sew Welcome. Mary Ann and Sadie were both there, preparing to open for the day.

"Think it will be busy today?" Liz asked, pausing to regard a display of fat quarters with a Thanksgiving theme. In one swatch, cute Pilgrims worked in a pumpkin patch. In another, turkeys held signs claiming they were stuffed.

"I sure hope so." Sadie slid bolts of fabric back into place. "I put a sandwich sign up in the square directing people this way. Maybe some of the craft-fair attendees will feel inspired to make their own projects."

"We usually do pretty well when there's an event in town. People like to check out the stores." Mary Ann glanced at the clock. "Liz, do you have time to run me to the garage? My car is in the shop, and they said it was ready."

Liz checked the time too. She had an hour before the craft fair started. "Sure, I can do that."

A few minutes later, Liz pulled up in front of the inn.

Mary Ann hurried out and slid into the passenger seat. "Thanks for doing this. I hope I can make it back before we open."

"I'll do my best." Liz put the Acura in drive, and they were off. Downtown was already jammed with traffic, so Liz took a side street. "Where to?"

"Stevens' Motors. That's on the edge of town."

Liz made another turn that would take them in the correct direction. "That's right. I remember you saying that your car was being repaired at Stevens.'"

"I always go there." Mary Ann gazed out the window at the passing houses, some already sporting Christmas decorations. "I love this time of year. I'm going to put up my lights this weekend."

Liz felt a pang of dismay. "This early? I haven't even begun to think about it." She liked to decorate a nicely shaped evergreen tree in the front yard as well as trim the eaves, doors, and windows. She also set an electric candle in each window, an old-fashioned touch that suited the inn.

Shiny rows of cars and trucks parked under strings of triangular flags flapping in the breeze announced the dealership. Liz pulled into the wide drive and drove up to the front door, which led into the showroom and office. She shut off the engine. "I'll come in and make sure your car is ready."

Mary Ann paused with her hand on the door handle. "You don't have to do that. They said it was fixed."

"You never know. I don't want to leave you stranded." She recalled a time or two when she had arrived at a garage and learned the person who phoned had jumped the gun. Liz opened her own door and followed Mary Ann into the building.

Tiffany Blake, the young woman Liz had met at the quilt shop, sat behind a desk near the entrance. Behind her were a couple of glass-windowed offices and a few chairs serving as a waiting area, and to her right, a couple of new cars were parked on platforms.

"May I help you?" Tiffany set aside a textbook titled *Foundations of Chemistry*. Several other thick books stood in a stack on the desk. Liz remembered her own college days and the pressure to study whenever and wherever she could.

Mary Ann explained her errand, and Tiffany leafed through a stack of invoices in a tray on the corner of the desk. "Here you go."

"What do I . . . ?" When Mary Ann glanced at the total, her words trailed off, and her eyes widened in outrage. "Five hundred dollars? This is way more than what I was quoted."

Tiffany shrugged, chomping on a piece of gum. "I have no idea. I just total the numbers they give me."

Mary Ann checked the bill again, talking to herself as she added the numbers. Then she shook the piece of paper at Tiffany. "I demand to see the manager."

The receptionist's gaze darted back and forth. "I think he's out. You'll have to come back another time."

Mary Ann pointed with a shaking finger at one of the offices, and Liz saw a man seated behind a desk, partially hidden by the blinds. "He's right there." She planted both hands on the desk, looming over Tiffany, who slid her chair back with a squeak. "I'm staying here until you call him and tell him I want to see him."

Never having witnessed the normally tranquil Mary Ann in a temper before, Liz gawked at her friend in amazement.

Indecisive, Tiffany plucked at her lip, but Mary Ann didn't budge. Finally, the young woman heaved a big sigh and picked up the phone. "Kevin, there's a customer here to see you. Mary Ann Berne." A man's low tones came through the receiver. "She won't take no for an answer." Another rumble. "Okay, I will." She slammed down the receiver and jerked her thumb at the office door. "Go on in."

Mary Ann stormed by.

Before following her friend, Liz thanked Tiffany, who already had her nose in the textbook again.

Inside the office, a lanky man looked up from his desk as they entered. Liz recognized Kevin Fiske, pointed out to her by Jackson at the football game. He, too, sported a black eye. He gave them a toothy grin. "What can I do for you lovely ladies today?"

Mary Ann snorted in answer as she thrust the invoice at him. "For starters, you can change the bottom line on this bill." As Kevin perused it, she said, "I didn't authorize that work. My car was supposed to be in for a tune-up and an oil change."

Liz started, unaware of the small scope of the ordered services. No wonder Mary Ann was steamed.

Kevin sat back in his chair and swiveled. Then he picked up a small desk calendar, the kind of thing given out for promotion. He handed it to Mary Ann. "See our slogan?"

Mary Ann stared down at the calendar, and Liz moved to read it over her shoulder. *Stevens' Motors: When it comes to service, we stand for safety first*, it said along the bottom.

"What's this got to do with anything?" Mary Ann practically flung the calendar into the middle of his desk blotter.

"You wouldn't want us to let your car leave the shop in a dangerous condition, would you?" Kevin appeared somber. "Your ball joints were ready to let go."

Mary Ann sank into a chair. "What does that mean?"

"Ball joints hold the front wheels on. When they fail, your steering wheel doesn't work." Kevin demonstrated twisting a wheel with a horrified expression. "Your wheels wobble, and boom, you go off the road." He shook his head. "I've seen quite a few fatalities due to bad ball joints."

Although Liz knew Kevin was laying on the fear factor, she felt a stab of alarm. How were *her* ball joints?

Mary Ann snatched the bill with a growl. "I guess I'd better go pay this then." Without another word to Kevin, she stalked out of the room.

Liz hurried to catch up. "Are you all set?" she asked.

"I am. Thanks for bringing me." Mary Ann slapped down a credit card for Tiffany to run. She leaned over to Liz and whispered, "But I'm never coming back."

Claudia Stevens bustled through the door, attractive in a skirt suit, and greeted Mary Ann and Liz. "How are you today?"

Mary Ann slid her credit card back into her wallet. "I've been better." She signed the slip with a flourish and handed it to Tiffany. "Take a look at this." She presented her copy of the bill to Claudia.

Claudia studied the page, puzzled. "What am I looking at?"

"Unauthorized work. And if I hadn't had the money, I'm sure Kevin would have held my car hostage."

Claudia crumpled the bill in her fist, apparently before she realized what she was doing. She smoothed it out and gave it back to Mary Ann. "I'm really sorry about this. They didn't call you before doing the job?"

"No, they didn't." Mary Ann tossed the bill into her purse and turned to Liz. "Ready to go?" She marched out of the dealership, Liz on her heels. "I'll see you later. Thanks again."

"No problem." As Liz got into her car, she glanced through the plate glass windows. Claudia was talking to Tiffany, her body language revealing that she was angry. Tiffany had her head down and her shoulders hunched in the classic posture of someone enduring a scolding. Then the dealership owner beelined to Kevin's office and threw open the door without knocking.

No one is happy if the boss isn't happy. Liz put the car in gear and started off. On the way back to town, she passed the road where her cousin and Sarah's mother-in-law lived with her family. On an impulse, she turned that way. The craft fair could wait.

Liz enjoyed driving through the countryside, and even at that time of year, when the fields lay dormant and the trees were losing their leaves, it had a tranquil beauty that restored her heart. With a feeling of coming home, Liz turned into the Borkholder driveway and parked in front of the big white house.

Once the family connection had been established, the friendship between Liz and Miriam had blossomed into almost a sisterhood. Despite the differences in their cultures, the Borkholders made Liz feel like part of a warm, loving clan, something she had never experienced in a somewhat lonely childhood.

Miriam answered the door. "How nice to see you." Her serene, indigo eyes lit with pleasure. "Come on in and have a cup of coffee. I've just made a pot."

Liz accepted the invitation with a laugh. "Good timing on my part."

"What brings you out here?" Miriam asked as she led the way to the neat kitchen. She gestured for Liz to sit at the long pine table.

"I took Mary Ann to pick up her car at the shop, and after I dropped her off, I decided on the spur of the moment to come and see you." Liz left the story at that, not planning to gossip about Mary Ann's problems at the business.

As Miriam poured coffee and set out milk and sugar, they chatted about the inn and the Pleasant Creek Thanksgiving event. Although the Amish didn't participate in many English celebrations, they sold traditional crafts, furniture, and food to visitors and locals alike.

"Will you be joining us for Thanksgiving this year?" Miriam asked.

Disappointment at not being able to spend the holiday with the Borkholders struck Liz anew. "It's so nice of you to ask, but didn't Sarah tell you?"

"She didn't." Miriam pressed her lips together. "You must not say no. You are family."

"It's not that. I'm hosting a dinner for my guests, so I'll have to miss your meal."

"What time is your dinner?" Miriam got up and grabbed the coffeepot.

"Midday. One or two o'clock, probably." Liz laughed. "I'll be up at dawn putting the turkey in the oven." Or later, depending on its size. She still didn't have a final head count.

Miriam filled Liz's cup and then her own. "There is not a problem. We eat later in the evening. So serve your guests and then come eat with us."

Joy bubbled up in Liz's heart. She wasn't going to be alone on the holiday after all. "I'll be there. I promise."

Liz took another detour on the way back to town, following Miriam's advice to reserve a turkey now. "They go fast," Miriam had said. "The Masts may not even have any left."

Now, as Liz slowed on the rutted dirt road leading to the Mast farm, she pondered what size to order. She still didn't know if Connie's and Ron's children would be joining them. It was better to buy one that was too large, she decided. She could freeze the leftover meat for potpies, tetrazzini, and soup. *I'll be eating turkey all the way until Christmas.*

A farmhouse, barns, and what looked like poultry houses appeared on the left. As Liz drew closer, she saw flocks of turkeys in a large pen, their enormous white bodies jostling each other for the grain a young Amish man was tossing.

A sign swung from a post in front of the farmhouse, and Liz slowed down even more to read it. Mast Poultry Farm. This was it then. Smaller letters below the name read, Elmo Mast, Proprietor.

Elmo. The name Piper had doodled over and over. *It has to be a coincidence, right?*

6

Liz found a spot to park in the barnyard, next to a couple of other cars. The Mast farm was a popular place. With a sense of urgency, she got out of the car and rushed toward the big red barn. Through a glass-paned door, she spotted a few people gathered in front of a counter, behind which an Amish man stood.

"All set for the big day?" A man in front of Liz asked the farmer. "Or should I say, are your turkeys ready?" He turned to his wife. "They're probably planning their escape as we speak."

The Amish man, who appeared to be about Liz's age, gave his customer a patient smile. Liz was sure he'd heard all the jokes. "What size turkey do you want to order, ma'am?"

The woman consulted her list. "I'm not sure. I never remember how many pounds per person I should get."

"How many people are eating?" From his tone, Liz was sure he asked this question dozens of times a day.

"Well, let's see. I've got the five kids coming and their families, so that's . . . and us of course. Eighteen," she announced proudly. "Almost forgot one of the babies."

"He won't be eating turkey yet, Madge," her husband said. "Maybe some mashed potatoes."

"That's true. So seventeen."

"I recommend a twenty-pounder. You will have a few leftovers, but that is better than running out."

"Perfect. Thanks." The woman spelled out her name and address, paid for the bird, and the couple turned to leave.

By the time Liz reached the counter, she was prepared. "I want a twelve-pound bird for six or seven guests and lots of leftovers."

With raised brows and a tiny smile of appreciation, the man wrote up the order. "Name and address?"

Liz gave him the information, then asked, "Are you Elmo? I saw the name on the sign." She found some bills in her wallet.

He handed her change. "I am afraid not. Elmo is my father. I am Ezra Mast."

"And I'm Liz Eckardt. Which you already know." She giggled as she gestured at the order form. The formal manners displayed by many Amish still made Liz feel slightly awkward. "Anyway, I operate the Olde Mansion Inn."

"Very nice. A beautiful house."

"It is. Sarah Borkholder works for me." Liz was determined to make connections with her new neighbors—with respect for their caution and reticence, of course.

He nodded. "I know the Borkholders."

"Yes, you came highly recommended by them and many others in town."

The younger man Liz had seen feeding the turkeys entered through a back door into the barn proper. "*Grossvater* is asking for you. I'll take over here."

"Thank you, *Sön*." Ezra rounded the counter, joining Liz as she exited. At her sympathetic, questioning glance, he said, "*Vater* is not doing well."

Liz knew he meant his father. "I'm sorry. Is he sick?"

"Very sick." Ezra's expression was gloomy. "He is not expected to recover."

Liz felt shock at this dire news. "I'm so sorry to hear that." She paused. *Should I? Oh, why not? It can't hurt.* "I will pray for him. For Elmo's recovery."

"Thank you. I—we—appreciate that." With a nod of farewell, he turned toward the house.

Saddened by Ezra's news, Liz headed back into town. She had lost both of her parents, and she prayed sincerely that Elmo would get better and be able to enjoy the holidays with his family.

That thought reminded her again of Steve, who so rarely made it home since he'd joined the military. *At least I've got some family here.* No one would or could ever replace Steve in her affections, but she couldn't deny the comfort of being near people she loved. *Maybe after he's discharged, he'll move here.* Imagining that very special event kept her occupied until she reached the inn. Her plan was to park there and walk down to the town square where the craft fair was being held.

As she started along the sidewalk, she heard snatches of music from the craft fair and quickened her steps in response. Although the temperature was in the low fifties, the sun was warm and the sky bright blue. It was a lovely, crisp day for an outdoor event, and the setting was much nicer than the school gymnasium that had been reserved in case of rain.

Greeting friends and neighbors heading in both directions, to and from the fair, Liz reached the square, which was lined with small booths on all four sides. From food trucks parked nearby came delightful smells of grilling sausage, homemade doughnuts, and brewing coffee.

A display of handmade yarn items caught her eye, and she bought Steve a striped scarf. He'd get a kick out of its bold design, and it would keep him warm in the winter, like a cozy hug sent thousands of miles.

Another booth held beeswax candles, and Liz purchased half a dozen pine-scented ones for the inn. They would be a nice touch this time of year. She also selected a fat column candle in a vanilla-lavender scent to burn while lounging in the bathtub, one of her favorite indulgences.

Thankful that she'd brought a tote to hold her acquisitions, Liz moved along to Christmas ornaments. She picked out a gorgeous blown-glass angel ornament, resolving to start a tradition of buying a new ornament each year. Then she selected two more for Mary Ann and Sadie.

And I'd better get the Christmas lights out of the attic this afternoon. After making that mental note, she found a table with a good view of the fair and sat down with a sausage sandwich smothered with condiments and a bottle of apple cider. Nearby, a bluegrass band played seasonal favorites with a country flair.

Chief Houghton strolled up to her table. "Finding some good things to buy?"

Finishing her juicy bite, she nodded. "I'm making quite a dent in my Christmas list."

"Glad to hear it." The chief glanced around, keeping an eye on the crowd.

"You're not expecting another brawl, are you?" Liz's question was tongue in cheek. A more placid, happy throng would be hard to find.

He shot her a sharp look. "Heard about that, did you?"

"Of course. One of the participants is staying at my inn. Tony Lee." Liz pointed at Tony, who was near the merry-go-round filming, Piper standing beside him.

"Oh yes, I remember him. He got caught up in the action. At least that's what he said."

"I believe him. He's a stranger here and couldn't possibly have an ax to grind. Not like Bob and Kevin, apparently." Liz paused. "Tony said Bob threatened Kevin."

The chief shrugged it off. "Bob was blowing off steam; that's all. He and Kevin have been at each other since they were in school."

Liz took another bite. After she swallowed, she asked casually, "What caused it? The two of them being enemies, I mean."

Houghton hooked both thumbs in his belt, shifting from leg to leg. "I'm not exactly sure. Back when they were younger, Bob was one of those kids who had it all. Looks, money, sports championships, the whole bit. Kevin came from the wrong side of the tracks, shall we say, and he always had a chip on his shoulder. The two of them clashed from the get-go."

"Over Claudia, maybe?" Liz guessed.

"Could be. Although Bob dated someone else quite seriously. Connie Gregg, her name is now."

"She's also a guest at the inn this week. She and her new husband, Ron." Liz and the chief exchanged amused smiles, both equally impressed with the other's grasp of local gossip, Liz supposed.

"Not that I like to gossip," the chief said, confirming Liz's theory, "but I find it pays to keep informed about what's going on. You never know when a situation's going to blow up into a problem."

"Like it did last night," Liz said.

"That's right." The chief narrowed his eyes, chewing on his lip. "Life's funny sometimes. Now the situation with Bob and Kevin is reversed. Kevin's riding high, and Bob... well, Bob isn't doing too good."

A thought struck Liz. "Where did Kevin get the money to invest in the dealership? It sounds like he didn't come from a wealthy background."

"You know, that's a good question. Kevin lived in Chicago for decades, ever since he went to college on a scholarship. He must have made it big there and cashed out to come home. A lot of people do that—come home later in life."

"I can understand that. I loved Boston, but I love Pleasant Creek more." Liz grinned at the chief.

"I'm glad you do." Houghton tipped his hat. "I'd better get on. Have a good day. And don't spend too much money."

Liz rolled rueful eyes. "Oh, I will. Have a good day yourself, Chief."

He strode away, and Liz turned her attention to her lunch, thinking about what else she wanted to browse. A nearby booth sold spices and, judging by the aroma drifting her way, mulled cider mix. She decided she should pick up some and brew a batch.

A woman carrying a tote bag cut through the crowd, and as she drew closer, Liz noticed it was Claudia Stevens. *Doing a little lunchtime shopping, perhaps?*

Claudia spotted Liz, then changed her course and approached her with a wave. "Liz Eckardt, you're just the person I want to see."

7

Liz stared up at Claudia in surprise. How could she possibly help the business owner? She hoped it wasn't anything to do with a possible campaign against Jackson. That would be a definite no.

Without invitation, Claudia pulled out the chair opposite Liz and sat down, setting her bag on the ground. "By the look on your face, you're wondering what on earth I'm talking about."

Liz laughed. "I'm afraid I am. Fire away."

Claudia leaned forward. "You know I'm the final judge for the pie Baking Bonanza?"

It wasn't about Jackson. Liz gave a tiny sigh of relief. "I didn't know that, but I heard that you sponsored it. Very generous of you."

Claudia flushed, pressing her lips together with pleasure. "Thanks. All the proceeds are going to charity. That's why, when we got news that our winners could qualify for nationals, I said bring it on." She smiled. "The number of contestants skyrocketed."

"That's great news." Then Liz guessed where this was headed. "But it means a bigger crowd to handle and more help is needed."

"Bingo." Claudia pointed a manicured finger at Liz. "You see, we'll need many judges for the first round, which will narrow down the entries to five. Then I will judge those and choose a winner."

Imagining the ire of the four losers, Liz was thankful not to be involved with the final round. "I do have a friend entering. Mary Ann Berne."

An irritated look crossed Claudia's face at the mention of Mary Ann. Was she annoyed at her former customer or at her employees? "All the entries will be numbered, and none of the judges will see the list until the contest is over. So you should be able to remain objective." She bared her teeth in what passed for a smile. "If you think it will be a problem, let me know now."

"It shouldn't be. I've never had Mary Ann's pumpkin pie." Liz made a note not to even look at Connie's pies, let alone taste them. Bias in either case would be impossible to avoid.

"Good." Claudia reached into her tote bag and pulled out a stapled stack of photocopied papers. "These are the rules and judging criteria. Read them over before the contest." After Liz accepted the paperwork, Claudia slapped the table and rose. "We're all set." She told Liz the time to show up for the contest and then bustled away, stopping to buttonhole someone else, Liz saw with amusement. Claudia would track down enough judges, no doubt of that.

Back at the inn, Liz stopped at Sew Welcome to say hello to Mary Ann and Sadie. The shop was in a lull, with only one customer browsing the supplies.

"How was the craft fair?" Sadie asked. Once again, she was organizing bolts of cloth, a sign of a busy day.

"I found all kinds of things. Want to see?" Liz put her tote on the counter, where Mary Ann was tallying slips. She pulled out the scarf, the candles, and the mulled cider mix for them to admire. The angel ornaments stayed in their boxes, hidden from view.

"I'd like to go to the fair for a few minutes," Sadie said. "Is that all right, Mary Ann?"

"Sure, go ahead. I can handle it." Mary Ann turned to the customer, who brought up an armload of supplies to buy. "Are you ready?"

Wanting to give Mary Ann the update on the pie contest, Liz packed away her craft fair purchases and lingered, looking over the holiday-themed cottons. A green fabric printed with hand-drawn golden squash and orange pumpkins cried out to become napkins for her table. She mentally counted the days remaining before Thanksgiving. Napkins were quick—just cut and hem. She could do it, she decided.

After the customer left, Liz hauled the bolt of fabric to the cutting table. "I'd like to buy some of this. Enough for a dozen napkins."

"Nice choice." Mary Ann calculated the yardage, then unfolded the cloth, lining it up against the gauge. "I thought of a great tweak to my pumpkin pie recipe." She gave Liz a rueful smile. "Maybe I can recoup my car repair expense if I win."

Liz put up a hand. "Hold on before you say anything else. Claudia asked me to be a judge, and I said yes."

Mary Ann pulled a finger across her lips. "I won't say another thing." Her eyes glinted. "But I bet my improvements will make all the difference."

"I hope they do. But you're a shoo-in anyway. I love your pies."

"You're sweet to say so." Mary Ann bent her head over the table, shears flashing as she expertly cut the fabric. "I'm trying to be philosophical about it. May the best pie win and all that."

"That's a good attitude," Liz said, "but I still think you'll win."

"I hope you're right." Mary Ann regarded the cut piece of cloth. "How about I go ahead and cut your napkins? It will only take a minute."

"Would you? That will save me a lot of work." Liz watched in admiration as Mary Ann measured and cut all twelve napkins, then stacked them neatly and carried them to the register.

As Liz was paying, a group of three women came into the shop, chattering away about quilting projects. Liz grabbed her things, thanked

Mary Ann, and beat a hasty retreat. The quilt shop, like all businesses in Pleasant Creek, needed to make money when they could.

————— ///////////////////////// —————

The next day, Sunday, was quiet, and Liz relished the peace. After church, where she spontaneously invited Jackson over for supper, she made a big batch of beef stew, planning to freeze the leftovers for later. Her mother had taught her how to prepare this simple, tasty meal, first dredging the meat cubes in salted flour and then browning them in a heavy pan. Then she cut up carrots, potatoes, and onions, and added them to the pot along with broth. Her mother's special combination of spices came next, and Liz would add peas and corn later, once the rest of the stew had simmered into tenderness.

While the stew bubbled, emitting delicious odors, Liz sat down to sew the Thanksgiving napkins. By three o'clock, she had them stitched, pressed, and folded, ready for the celebration later in the week.

As she was coming out of the dining room, she ran into Connie, carrying two brown sacks of groceries. "There you are," her guest said. "I want to put my supplies in the kitchen for later when I bake."

"Of course." Liz led the way into the kitchen. "Go ahead and put the bags on the counter." She opened the fridge and made room on one of the shelves. "Feel free to use the fridge too."

"Thanks. I have a couple of things that need to go in there." Connie approached, holding a carton of eggs and a quart of cream. "I always use real cream instead of evaporated—oops, I forgot. You're one of the judges."

Liz put her hands over her ears with a laugh. "I didn't hear that. And I won't peek at your dry ingredients either." Then she thought of something. Connie needed to store her cooked pies in the fridge until the contest in the morning. How was she going to avoid seeing them? This judging thing was getting really complicated.

Ron entered the kitchen, holding a cardboard box in his arms. "I thought I'd find you two in here."

"You're just in time." Connie took the box and unpacked a mixing bowl, hand mixer, utensils, rolling pin, pie pans, and two plastic pie keepers. She held up one of the pie keepers. "Once the pies cool, they're going in here." She wagged a finger at Ron. "No peeking and no tasting."

"I won't peek or taste either. At least, not until tomorrow." Liz smiled, visions of pumpkin pies dancing in her head. Would she ever eat pumpkin again after this contest?

Ron snapped his fingers. "That's right. Connie said you're judging in the first round." He dug into his pocket and pulled out his wallet. "How much will it take for you to vote for her pie?" He wiggled his brows comically, letting Liz know he was joking.

Liz laughed. "I can't be bought."

"No bribing the judge." Connie finished arranging her baking supplies to her satisfaction, then turned to Liz. "When can I start?" She glanced at the steaming stew. "I don't want to interfere with your dinner."

"How about seven? We should be finished with the kitchen by then."

"Perfect." Connie looped her arm through her husband's and looked back at Liz. "See you later."

Since all her guests were out, Liz set a table in the main sitting room in front of the fireplace. One of her new pine candles burned on the mantel, and a cozy fire snapped and crackled. When she finished, she stood back, hands on hips, and admired the play of firelight on the crystal and china. Then she caught a glimpse of herself in a mirror across the room and yelped. She'd been so busy making the setting perfect that she'd forgotten to get ready.

Thankful the occasion was casual, Liz showered, then put on black pants and a soft, pink cashmere sweater. A brush through her hair and a swipe of lipstick, mascara, and blush, and she was all set.

Jackson rang the bell at six on the dot, punctual as always. When she opened the door, he thrust a big bouquet of fall flowers into her arms.

"These are lovely," Liz said, inhaling the spicy scent of mums. "You didn't have to bring me anything."

"My mother taught me to always bring a hostess gift," he said, shrugging out of his overcoat and running a hand through his wind-mussed hair. He glanced around, sniffing. "What smells so good?"

Just like a man to cut to the chase. "Beef stew and homemade bread." Liz walked toward the sitting room. "We're eating in here."

"This is nice." Jackson held his hands out to the fire. "It's getting chilly outside."

"I'm glad the cold weather held off for the craft fair." Liz arranged the flowers in a vase, then picked it up to fill it with water in the kitchen. "I'll be right back. Make yourself at home."

Jackson settled in an armchair by the fire while Liz took care of the flowers and then brought out glasses of tomato juice and a plate of cheese and crackers to nibble on before dinner.

While they chatted, Beans lumbered into the room to join them, plopping down on the hearth rug with a heavy sigh. He watched Jackson and Liz closely for dropped crumbs.

After they made a dent in the appetizers, Jackson helped Liz carry in big bowls of stew and a basket of crusty bread. They sat at the table, Jackson said grace, and they dug in.

"This is excellent," Jackson said. "The perfect meal on a blustery night."

As though underscoring his words, a heavy gust of wind buffeted the house, and rain dashed against the windows. The fire danced as wind whipped down the chimney.

"I didn't know it was supposed to rain."

"Me neither." He grinned at her. "It's nice being tucked up in front of the fire, isn't it?"

"It certainly is." Liz's cheeks felt hot. Was it the fire or the company?

The front door opened and shut, and Liz heard voices in the foyer. "Who could that be?" She pushed back from the table. At Jackson's puzzled look, she said, "I think I locked the door, but I don't remember."

The downside of being an innkeeper—constant interruptions. Liz rushed to the foyer where she saw Tony and Caitlyn taking off their coats. Both of them were drenched.

"Hi, Liz," Caitlyn said. "Tony and I planned to go out for dinner, but when we got there, we found out the restaurant is closed on Sundays." She swiped a hand through her short red-streaked hair. "It didn't used to be."

"We thought we'd regroup with cookies and coffee," Tony said. "And make another try somewhere else."

"Oh, I'm sorry. I didn't have coffee hour today, since no one was going to be here." Liz felt a twinge of guilt at their downcast faces and made the offer she knew she should. "But I did make plenty of beef stew. How does that sound?"

The couple exchanged grateful looks.

"Really? We don't want to intrude . . ." Caitlyn's voice trailed off.

Liz gestured. "Come on in. The more the merrier."

To his credit, Jackson merely smiled when Liz returned with guests in tow, then jumped up to pull out a leaf of the table and locate two more chairs. Liz and Caitlyn set the places, and they all sat down to eat.

Once again, Liz noticed what a sociable young man Tony was. He kept the conversation hopping with anecdotes of his travels around Pleasant Creek filming footage for the show. His tale of how a garrulous old-timer wanted to keep talking . . . and talking . . . on camera made them roar with laughter.

"You're doing a lot of shooting, and the contest hasn't even been held yet," Liz remarked.

"We only use tiny pieces of all those scenes to make a collage. To give a feel for the place." Tony turned to Jackson. "You're the mayor, right?"

"Yes, I am." Jackson winked at Liz. "This term anyway."

"I think we should get you on camera for the show."

Jackson patted his chest. "Me? I don't do anything with pies except eat them."

Tony shifted to sit on the edge of his seat, his dark hair practically standing on end with excitement. "That's even better. We'll show you eating a piece of the winning pie at the close of the show."

"That would be fabulous, Jackson," Caitlyn said. "Maybe they'll let you use the clip on the town and chamber websites."

With an impish smile, Liz jumped in. "It would be great promotion, right?" Of course, Claudia wouldn't be pleased to have her rival share the spotlight, but that wasn't Liz's fight to referee.

"*Et tu, Brute?*" Jackson struck a pose, squaring his shoulders. "Something like this?" He deepened his voice. "Welcome to Pleasant Creek, where we bake award-winning pies and . . . and . . ." In his regular voice, he said, "I guess I better work on my lines."

Beans, still lying by the fire, rolled over and gave a long, rasping snore capped by a snort. He shook his head, rattling his tags, then sank into slumber again.

Everyone burst into laughter.

Jackson said, "Typical constituent. Every time I speak, they go to sleep."

They all laughed again.

"Don't feel bad. Everything puts Beans to sleep." Liz pushed back her chair. "Anyone want decaf? And I'll see if I can rustle up some cookies."

On the way to the kitchen, Liz heard the front door open and turned back to see who was there.

Piper came in and bolted for the stairs, shedding her coat as she went.

"Want to join us for coffee and cookies?" Liz offered.

Piper shook her head, and when Liz looked closer, she noticed her guest was fighting tears. "I'm sorry . . . I just can't right now." She thundered up the stairs.

Liz watched her go. *What was that all about?*

8

"Smile, everyone. That's it." Piper stood back and motioned for Tony to film the group of judges standing in front of the Order of the Otter Lodge.

Liz stretched her mouth in a smile, hoping she wouldn't blink or make a strange face while the camera was trained on her face. Piper looked fine this morning, Liz reflected, a little wan but not unhappy as she corralled people into place. Whatever she had been crying about the previous night appeared to have either been resolved or tucked away.

Beyond Piper and Tony, other reporters and a television news truck were gathered, present to cover what apparently was a newsworthy event. Piper's food show was already bringing new attention to the town.

A steady stream of contestants entered through a side door, carefully carrying their precious cargo of two pies each. Liz spotted Mary Ann, her cheeks bright with excitement, and Connie, who made Ron transport her entries, barking advice at him all the way from the car to the entrance.

Jackson strode down the sidewalk, handsome in a suit jacket and pressed slacks.

When Piper saw him, she called out, "Glad you could make it, Mr. Mayor. Go stand in front of the judges."

Claudia, standing in the center of the group, frowned. "What's he doing here? This is my event."

Jackson shrugged. "They wanted to include me as a representative of Pleasant Creek. I promise I'm not trying to steal your thunder."

Claudia's face softened slightly at his ingratiating smile, and she moved aside an inch or two to make room, allowing Jackson to stand beside her, not in front.

"Ready when you are, Jackson," Tony said from behind the lens.

Jackson straightened his tie and cleared his throat. "As mayor of this fine town, I'd like to welcome you all to A Pleasant Creek Thanksgiving and today's pumpkin pie Baking Bonanza. Thanks to the generosity of local business owners such as Claudia Stevens, standing beside me, our contestants have a shot at a national prize." Dropping the formality, Jackson pumped his fist into the air. "Go, Pleasant Creek pie bakers!"

The line of judges followed suit, pumping fists and yelling, "Go, Pleasant Creek!"

Tony moved in closer, and Liz noticed the television news camera was also focused on them. They'd probably make the evening news. A thrill of exhilaration traveled up her spine. This was going to be fun, and she was glad to be part of it.

"All right, judges, ready, set, go!" Claudia shouted.

"May the best pie win," they chanted in unison as previously directed, then turned as one and marched into the building in single file.

Jackson stepped out of the queue, and as Liz passed, he whispered, "Don't eat too much."

She grinned. "Now you warn me." Actually, in anticipation of sampling many pies, she'd had only coffee and juice for breakfast. She was downright hungry.

Inside the building, the main hall was set up with long tables for the first round of pies. Rows of folding chairs were filling fast with contestants and their supporters. Liz recognized Sadie's flowered purple hat bobbing as she bent to talk to a neighbor. Near the other entrance, Tiffany, the young woman from the auto dealership, was in charge of contestant intake, assigning each baker a number and passing the numbered pies through into the kitchen.

Liz and the other judges were whisked into a side room, where they would remain until the contest got under way. Carafes of ice water were the only refreshments available, and Liz poured herself a cup.

"I heard they cut off the entries at fifty," a balding, middle-aged man said to Liz. "We're going to have to taste ten pies per team."

Liz counted the other judges; there were ten including her, so pairing up, yes, they would sample ten pies each. "And each team picks a winner? Wow, that's going to be hard."

"It sure is." The man sounded gloomy. "My sister entered, and I really hope they don't give me her slice of pie or I'll never hear the end of it."

"You wouldn't pick hers?"

He shook his head morosely. "Not in a million years. She's a terrible cook." He smacked his lips. "Her crust is like tough cardboard, and her filling is watery."

Liz bit back a laugh. *Maybe the competition isn't so steep after all.* Mary Ann probably had a really good chance of winning.

Then another woman spoke up. "My friend is a three-time state winner. Her crust is to die for, and she's really creative with her spices." When Claudia glared at her, she quickly added, "But I made her promise not to tell me what she's doing for this contest."

Claudia sighed. "Folks, I know it's going to be hard to avoid tasting pie made by someone you know. That's why I'm going to pair you up carefully. And all team votes must be unanimous. If we need a tiebreaker, I'll bring in another judge."

"How about our mayor?" a woman called out. "He'd be perfect." She was joined by several other shouts of approval.

Claudia's mouth turned down at the mention of Jackson. "I'll think about it. Let's just try to avoid the problem, okay?"

Liz's stomach churned in anticipation—and not in a good way. How were her taste buds going to be able to differentiate between ten pies and pick a clear winner? Strange to say, she hoped a good number of them—nine for instance—would be easy to reject.

She was paired with the dour man hoping to avoid his sister's pie, and after what seemed an interminable wait, they were ushered out into the main room. Cheers and applause greeted them as the audience surged to their feet.

Nothing like a little pressure.

"Go, Liz!" someone yelled.

Liz glanced over to see the Material Girls sitting together—Opal Ringenberg and Naomi Mason along with Mary Ann, Sadie, and Caitlyn. Chief Houghton and Officer Jack Gerst were on hand. Crowd control, Liz supposed.

Clutching clipboards, Liz and her new friend Theo were herded to a table on the left. Here ten pies sat, an array of baked goodness, for the most part. Liz did spot a burned crust here and a less-than-consistent filling there. Although standard pumpkin pies accounted for half the entries, pumpkin meringue, pumpkin cranberry, pumpkin cream pie, swirly pumpkin cheesecake, and one labeled pumpkin habanero made up the rest. A volunteer stood behind the table, pie server at the ready.

"All right, judges," Claudia said. She'd already given the spiel in the other room, but this was for the benefit of the audience and the television cameras, the local station having joined Piper and Tony inside. "You see before you the pie entries you will be judging. First you look at the presentation of the whole pie and grade it for eye appeal, one to ten, with ten being worthy of a cooking show."

The audience laughed as Claudia glanced at Piper, standing beside her.

"That's right, Claudia," Piper said. "There are some gorgeous pies waiting to be sampled here today." Tony panned the tables, zooming in on the pretty pies. "It's hard to believe these are amateur creations. Some of them are quite unusual."

"All we required is that the pie have crust and contain pumpkin," Claudia said. "Although, many entries are traditional pies, as you can see." She smiled. "But I'm sure there are some surprises. Don't judge a pie by its looks."

Theo whispered to Liz, "I don't see my sister's pie here." He swiped his brow. "Phew."

Liz and Theo studied each entry on their table, writing down the number on the scoring sheet, then giving each a grade. When Liz was done, she had a couple of fives, two sixes, three sevens, an eight, a nine, and a ten. This last was pumpkin pie perfection, with a piping of whipped cream around the edge of the uniform crust, like a frill.

"Now that you've judged the whole pie, the real test begins," Claudia said. "Do these pies taste as good as they look? That is the question."

Again the crowd laughed.

"On your mark, get set, serve!"

The attendants behind each table deftly sliced the pies, then served one piece from each onto plates and set them in a row. Again, Liz and Theo minutely examined each pie, judging its appearance.

A couple of entries were easy to eliminate, due to the filling slumping out of the crust into a gooey pile. Another was so firm Liz guessed that a lot of cornstarch or gelatin had been used to make the piece resemble plastic.

The attendant had set out plain crackers and glasses of water for the judges to ingest between samples. Two forks were placed beside each sample.

"Are you ready?" Theo asked Liz. His face was grimly determined.

Liz took a deep breath. "Ready as I'll ever be."

One by one, they moved down the line of pies, taking bites of the tip and crust. Savor, taste, chew, swallow. Make notes, then drink a sip of water and eat a cracker. On to the next.

By the last entry, Liz felt like a pie-tasting machine. She concentrated on each mouthful, trying to determine the blend of flavors used, the level of sweetness, how the filling felt in her mouth. Eating pie would never be the same mindless pleasure it had been in the past.

The last entry she tasted was also the one that Liz had ranked ten for presentation. Hoping she wasn't too jaded, she cut off the tip and popped it into her mouth. It was the perfect blend of spicy and sweet. It was smooth and not too sticky or watery. The ultimate pumpkin pie.

The crust was equally good—melt-in-your-mouth flaky, like fine pastry should be. It was the kind of crust you could eat plain if you wanted.

She caught Theo's eye, and he gave a tiny nod. "This is it," he said. "Our entry for the next round."

Liz set her clipboard down, glad the judging had been so easy. A couple of the others were close and, depending on preferences, could have been winners had it not been for entry number 38, the tenth one on their list.

Other teams weren't having such an easy time. At one table, an argument had broken out, with one judge avowing that only plain pie should win. The other judge pointed to a sky-high whipped confection. "This is my winner," she said.

Claudia put two fingers in her mouth and whistled. "Time

for a tiebreaker." She turned to Piper. "Ms. Reynolds, will you do the honors?"

"Me?" Piper put a hand to her chest as the crowd went wild. When the applause died down, she said, "I'll do it if you promise not to hold the results against me. My job depends on wrapping this segment, and I need your cooperation."

"Can we do it, everyone? Can Piper be honest with us?"

The audience shouted out the answer, punctuating their words with stamping feet.

"Yes, be honest."

"Tell the truth."

"Don't hold back."

Liz felt like she'd stepped onto the set of an especially lively game show. Claudia was certainly milking the drama for all it was worth.

Feigning great trepidation, Piper stepped over to the controversial entries, the cameras following. They zoomed in as she tasted one, then the other, sips of water in between. She thought, she deliberated, and she came to a decision. "The plain pie wins."

The spectators cheered while Tiffany gathered the winning entry's number. Fresh pies would be used in the next round for Claudia to judge. Next, Tiffany collected the rest of the winners, including entry number 38, and Claudia announced the bakers who were advancing to the next round. Liz's job was done.

Energetic music came over the loudspeakers as the contest adjourned briefly. The ladies' auxiliary of the Otters brought out platters of sandwiches, chips, and drinks to sell in a benefit for scholarships.

Liz joined the Material Girls.

"You should have seen your face once or twice," Sadie said. "Some of those pies weren't too good, huh?"

"It was a hard choice," Liz said, determined to be tactful. You never knew who was listening in a crowd this big in a town this small.

"Good job, Liz." Mary Ann appeared nervous. "I can't believe my pie made the final round."

"Congratulations," Liz said. "We chose number 38. A plain pie with whipped cream."

"I did a plain traditional pie with whipped cream." Mary Ann shrugged. "But they didn't tell us which number they gave us."

"Who wants lunch?" Opal asked. "I'll get some sandwiches."

"I'll help," Caitlyn said. She went around the circle taking orders, but Liz demurred.

"I can't eat anything." Liz rubbed her tummy. "Not for a while. Thanks though."

The other Material Girls settled back in their chairs to eat and wait for round two. Others in the audience did the same, although some of those who had been eliminated left, taking their family and friends with them. But new people filtered in, drawn by the drama of the exciting contest.

After about forty-five minutes, the music over the loudspeakers cut off and Jackson took the microphone. This was a pleasant surprise. "Good afternoon, ladies and gentlemen, pie lovers of Pleasant Creek. We're just about ready to start the final round of the pie contest." Everyone clapped. "First, a warm welcome to our lovely judge, Claudia Stevens."

Claudia emerged from the back room, waving and smiling.

Liz clapped along with everyone else. *Jackson is really laying it on thick. He is a good politician.*

"But, ladies and gentlemen, there's more. Claudia is the sponsor who made this contest possible. It's because of her generosity that one of our local bakers will be able to participate in the nationals. Give her another round of applause, everyone."

Claudia's cheeks flamed red at these accolades. "Thank you, all. It's been a pleasure. Now, are you ready to find out who the grand prize pie baker is?"

The throng assented with a mighty roar as attendants guided a large rolling cart out of the kitchen, the five pies in the final round riding proudly.

Even from here, Liz recognized entry 38's perfect shape and style, a classic pumpkin dream if she ever had seen one.

With great fanfare, Claudia worked her way through the pies, the audience hanging on every nuance of her expression as she tasted and contemplated, then made notes.

Number 38 was next to last. Sitting beside Liz, Mary Ann clutched her arm. Leaning close, she whispered, "That's my pie."

"It was superb," Liz whispered back. She patted Mary Ann's hand. "Good luck."

Claudia cut off the tip and popped it into her mouth, chewing thoughtfully. The crust bite was next, a perfect blend of crust, filling, and fluffy cream. Again, Claudia munched slowly. Then her eyes widened, and she dropped her fork.

While everyone watched in stunned disbelief, not quite sure what was happening, the judge started choking and collapsed to the floor, writhing and arching her back. Her strangled breath broke the silence in the quiet room. Screams rippled through the audience.

Mary Ann surged to her feet. "That's my pie!" she cried out.

9

Liz and almost everyone else in the room jumped to their feet. With murmured excuses, Caitlyn edged past the others and ran toward the stricken woman, kneeling to help. Chief Houghton and Officer Gerst rushed to join Caitlyn, the chief speaking into his shoulder microphone, summoning an ambulance.

"That's my pie," Mary Ann repeated. "Maybe she was allergic to one of the ingredients."

"Don't assume it was your pie that caused this." Sadie's tone was gruff. "She might be having a delayed reaction to the car accident. Or she could be having a heart attack."

In Liz's mind, the symptoms Claudia was displaying didn't fit either scenario. Claudia was showing signs of being poisoned. But how could that be? Surely one of those beautiful pies couldn't be the cause. Until an hour ago, no one had known which ones were going to be selected for the final round.

Voices around them rose in confusion as Claudia remained on the floor; Caitlyn's efforts didn't seem to help. Liz dug her fingernails into her palms, praying that Claudia would be all right. By Mary Ann's bowed head and folded hands, Liz guessed she was doing the same.

"Stand back! Stand back!" Chief Houghton shouted.

Three EMTs pushed through with a gurney, forcing standing, chattering onlookers to move out of the way.

The chief's searching gaze landed on Officer Gerst. "Establish a perimeter and move these folks to the back of the room."

Gerst hurried to obey. "Okay, folks, let's move back and give the EMTs room."

Tony stopped filming, but the news crew camera kept running as the officer ushered them to the back of the room.

The EMTs bent over Claudia, assessing her vitals, starting oxygen, and then loading her onto the gurney. The head medic conferred with the chief, whose expression grew grim.

As they wheeled her out, the crowd unanimously quieted, as if paying respect to the woman who only moments ago had been an engaging and charismatic master of ceremonies and judge. Liz noticed other officers filtering into the room, entering quietly to stand at the various exits. One went into the kitchen.

Once Claudia was gone and the wail of sirens faded into the distance, people began to mill about and talk, obviously not sure what to do. Some headed for the doors.

Chief Houghton went up to the microphone. After a few feedback squeals, which had the fortunate effect of attracting attention, he said, "The contest is canceled, ladies and gentlemen. However, no one is to leave the building until we say so."

Protests rippled through the room, and someone yelled, "Why not?"

"We need to speak to anyone who had access to the kitchen this morning," the chief answered.

Consternation arose as everyone began to speculate why—and who might be included in that roster.

"Quiet!" Chief Houghton commanded. "I also need to speak to the people whose pies made it into the final round."

Mary Ann sagged back into her chair. "I knew it. I knew it had something to do with my entry."

Sadie sat next to her and took her hand. "Hush. It will be okay."

A couple of women nearby glanced over in curiosity, whispering. Liz glared until they looked away.

"We don't know who those pies belong to," someone shouted. "Blind numbering."

Chief Houghton gestured for Tiffany to come forward with the master list. They matched up the numbers on the five pies with names, and the chief called out, "Mary Ann Berne, Connie Gregg . . ."

Liz didn't know the other contestants, two women and a man, but each reacted with shock, their friends and families gathering around them. Connie buried her head in Ron's shoulder.

"What is going on?" an elderly man asked in the row behind Liz. "What do the pies have to do with Claudia's illness?"

"They think she was poisoned," the woman beside him said. "It's obvious."

The rumor of poison spread through the crowd like wildfire.

"Maybe it's in the coffee," someone suggested.

"She didn't drink coffee," another person pointed out.

A woman nearby groaned and held her stomach. "I don't feel good. I shouldn't have had that sandwich."

The scene was about to turn into a riot of panic and fear. "Come on, ladies," Liz said. "Let's help." She stepped onto a chair, supported by Sadie and Naomi. Putting her fingers in her mouth, she gave the whistle that had fetched Steve home while playing three streets over. "Hey, people," she shouted when she had their attention. "Calm down and let Chief Houghton do his job. Anyone who didn't have access to the kitchen can leave, right, Chief?"

He cleared his throat and spoke into the mike. "Yes, that's right. Everyone who didn't go into the kitchen can leave, but the officers at the doors will be taking your names and phone numbers." He pointed to the far side of the room. "Those of you who worked in the kitchen, served food for sale, or had pies in the final round, wait over there, please."

Jackson waved his hand. "I went into the kitchen too."

At the chief's nod, Jackson joined Tiffany, the Otter Lodge ladies, Mary Ann, Connie, and the other contestants shuffling to the spot Houghton indicated. They huddled together like forlorn sheep.

The rest of the audience filed to the doors, stopping to give personal information. Smartly, the officers asked for identification from each, which slowed the process to a crawl but prevented someone from giving a false name. Liz and the others reluctantly left Mary Ann behind and joined the line to exit.

"I hate to leave Mary Ann here alone. I feel like I've thrown her to the wolves, but I'd better get back to the shop," Sadie said, glancing at her watch. "We closed for the contest, but I should open. I'm sure we're missing tons of sales."

"I'll be at the bakery," Naomi said. She owned Sweet Everything next to the inn. "But I'll be on edge until I hear what happens with Mary Ann. And poor Claudia, of course."

"We'll call you as soon as we learn anything," Liz said. "Promise."

Opal clasped her hands. "I'll be praying," the elderly woman said in her gentle voice. "For all concerned. And especially that Claudia pulls through."

"I sure hope she does." Sadie frowned. "Or else someone will be facing a murder charge."

Back at the inn, Liz couldn't settle. She flitted from room to room, straightening what was already perfectly in place, thanks to the efforts of Sarah, who had come and gone that morning.

A deep, gnawing suspicion told Liz the pies were the source of the poison. Claudia's symptoms came on rapidly after she began the tasting. But was it the first pie—or the last one she tried? And how had someone done it? For a moment she imagined that Claudia had done it to herself, a dramatic suicide on camera. But she dismissed that immediately. Despite the trauma of her divorce, the woman appeared happy. She was successful, admired, financially well-off, and a leader in town—someone who relished the spotlight.

And someone hated her enough to try to kill her. With success often came jealousy and enemies. Liz knew that firsthand, having faced opposition from professional rivals and from cliques in high school and college. She barely remembered the names of the girls who hadn't liked it when Liz won an award or dated a popular boy.

Could such enmity linger for decades? She recalled the disagreement between Claudia and Connie in the bathroom at the football game. Connie had lived in Indianapolis for over twenty years. The idea that their argument related to something that happened in high school seemed ludicrous. It had to be something more recent, like Claudia's divorce or even Connie's remarriage.

She replayed in her mind the words she'd overheard. *"You know the right thing to do. And you'd better do it."* And, *"Don't you threaten me. It didn't work then, and it won't work now."*

Who had made the threat? Liz racked her brain, trying to remember something, anything that would definitively identify the speakers. It was no use. Each time she replayed the memory it became more distorted.

The front door opened, and Liz peered out the sitting room door, expecting to see customers headed for Sew Welcome. But it was Connie and Ron.

Connie hurried toward her hostess. "I hope you can come with us to the hospital. We're holding a vigil for Claudia." She sighed deeply. "According to Bob, she's still hanging in there."

So Claudia's ex-husband is at the hospital. "I'd be happy to." Liz studied her guest closely, but she could only discern concern and worry for her old friend. "Any news from the police?"

Connie bit her lip, shaking her head. "I hate to tell you this, since I know you're friends and all." She glanced at the doorway of Sew Welcome and lowered her voice. "They're still questioning Mary Ann. Do you think . . . ?" Her voice trailed off.

"Now, Connie," Ron said, "don't start rumors."

His wife crossed her arms. "I'm not. It's a reasonable conclusion. They let me go, and my pie was second."

"What kind of pie did you make?" Liz asked.

"It was traditional, plain. No whipped cream." She sniffed. "If your pumpkin filling is good enough, whipped cream is a distraction from the flavor."

Mary Ann's pie had had whipped cream on it, as had one other. The last pie had been a crumb-topped confection. *Was the poison in the whipped cream? Or was it the timing of the symptoms that pointed to Mary Ann?* Liz chafed, wishing she knew more. In the meantime, she could do something useful by supporting Claudia.

"I'll get my keys," she said. "Meet you there."

———————— //////////////////////// ————————

The receptionist inside the main door of the hospital directed Liz to the correct floor, where she found Tiffany, Bob, and Kevin gathered in a small waiting room furnished with cloth-covered chairs and a rack of ancient magazines. On the wall, a television murmured at low volume.

"I can't believe this is happening," Tiffany moaned, then threw herself into Kevin's arms as best as she could in the confines of her chair.

Seated beside her, Kevin patted her back gingerly. "There, there. It's not over yet. She's still fighting."

Bob, who was leaning against the wall staring at the television, straightened when Liz walked in. Every time she saw him, he looked worse—unshaven, haggard, dark circles under his eyes. "Thanks for coming." He squinted at her in puzzlement. "Have we met?"

Liz thrust out her hand. "I don't think so. I'm Liz Eckardt, owner of the Olde Mansion Inn. Both Claudia and I are members of the chamber, and I was one of the judges today."

Bob shook her hand. "Oh, that's right. I remember seeing you at the contest."

Tiffany's sobs died to a sniffle. She glanced up at Liz as she crossed to take a seat. "Hello again." She gave Liz a feeble smile.

"I'm praying your boss will be all right."

"Thanks." Tiffany pulled a tissue out of her purse and blew her nose. "That's really nice of you."

"Kevin Fiske. I don't believe we've met. At least not officially." He stood and offered his hand to Liz. "Thanks for your support at this terrible time."

"Of course." Liz shook his hand, studying him closely. To all appearances, he looked and sounded sincere. Why, then, did the hackles stand up on her neck? Something about the man was off, just as it had been during the earlier encounter in his office.

Connie and Ron bustled into the room as Liz was taking a seat at the end of the row. "Any news?" Connie asked, glancing from person to person.

"I'm afraid not," Bob said. He stepped back when Connie engulfed him in a huge hug.

She burst into tears. "This is awful, so awful!" Her voice rose to a wail.

"It is." Bob glared over her shoulder at Kevin and Tiffany. "It is indeed."

Does he suspect them of trying to kill his ex-wife? The animosity between Kevin and Bob had led to blows only days ago. Liz wondered if it was business or personal—or both.

"Come on, dear," Ron said, detaching his wife from Bob. "Let's sit." He guided Connie to a chair, then asked, "Does anyone want coffee? I'll go to the cafeteria for some."

Liz was torn between staying for news—and watching the others—but she thought she should take advantage of the opportunity to speak to Ron alone. She didn't think she'd ever seen him without his wife hovering nearby. "I'll go and help you carry the coffees," she said. "Maybe I'll grab some snacks too."

"Oh, I can't eat a thing," Tiffany said.

"Neither can I," Connie chimed in. "I lose my appetite when I'm upset. During my divorce, I lost twenty pounds like that." She snapped her fingers.

In contrast, Kevin perked up. "I'll take a ham sandwich." He dug into his wallet and pulled out a few bills.

Liz and Ron trudged down the hall to the elevator, their shoes squeaking on the shiny tile. "Any news on your children?" Liz asked.

Ron shook his head. "Not yet. I'm sorry about that. There's only a couple more days until Thanksgiving, and I know it must be messing up your menu."

"No, I'm fine. I got a large turkey, so I'll freeze the leftovers." Liz pushed the button for the elevator.

Ron gestured at the rooms around them, the only noises the persistent *beep* of machines and quiet footsteps of medical personnel. "Something like this makes you realize just how short life is. I wish my kids would get that."

"Does anyone young ever understand that?"

"Probably not." Ron stood back to let Liz enter the elevator.

"But it's one of my personal philosophies. Life's too short to hold a grudge."

A belief that obviously the poisoner doesn't share. Liz seized the opening. "Then you think Claudia was definitely the target?"

"I have no idea." He shifted from foot to foot. "I was thinking of my kids—and Connie's—how they've been angry with us. And if something happened . . ."

"I understand." Liz studied the side of his face as he stared straight ahead at the elevator doors. "But the poison had to be meant for Claudia. None of the other judges got sick." She sighed. "Someone must really hate her."

He pressed his lips together, the tips of his ears reddening. "I don't want to speculate. That's up to the police to figure out."

Didn't want to speculate or afraid his wife might be implicated? Liz thought of Connie's long-standing dislike of the business owner. Was she the poisoner? If so, how had she done it?

The elevator slid to a stop, and the doors *dinged* open.

"Here we are." Ron's tone was hearty as he let her exit first. "Let's get some grub."

"I can smell the food cooking from here." Liz dropped the subject of Claudia. "All of a sudden, I'm starving."

It was another hour before the doctor entered the waiting room to share an update. Everyone shifted in their seats, almost identical looks of expectation and dread on their faces.

The doctor's gaze skipped around the room. "Is anyone here from the family?"

No one answered, and then Bob spoke up. "I guess I'm the closest thing. Her ex-husband."

"Bob Stevens?" The doctor checked over the records she held. "I see you're still listed as having permission to access Claudia's information."

"That's right." Bob's knee jiggled up and down in anxiety. "Please tell us how she is."

Liz was ready to scream too. She knew that hospital and medical providers had to follow rules about privacy, but in this case, procedures were a hindrance rather than a help.

The doctor smiled. "I'm happy to tell you that Claudia is going to be fine. It was touch and go for a while, but now she's stable and out of danger."

10

Liz exhaled in relief, the tension in her shoulders loosening. Claudia was going to live! She sent up a quick prayer of gratitude for this wonderful news.

The others in the room reacted in various ways, from Bob's heartfelt sigh to Tiffany's tears. Connie gave a yell of joy, then clapped a hand over her mouth.

Kevin rose, straightening his pant legs. "Can we see her, Doc?"

The doctor shook her head. "I'm afraid not. She's still very ill. Bob, as the next of kin, you can go in for five minutes."

Chief Houghton appeared in the doorway. "Hold on, Doctor. I'd rather keep Claudia in isolation right now until the results of the toxicology tests come back."

Liz's elation deflated slightly at this reminder that a criminal investigation was under way. She wondered how Mary Ann had fared in the interview and hoped the chief's request to bar visitors meant they hadn't narrowed suspicion down to her friend.

"As you wish, Chief," the doctor said.

"When will Claudia be released?" Tiffany moved to the edge of her chair. "Do you know?"

"I'm hoping in a couple of days," the doctor said. "It depends on how quickly the toxins clear from her system." She turned to the chief. "Can we speak in my office?"

A few minutes later as Liz followed the others out, she was relieved to see Officer Hughes in the hallway near Claudia's room. She hoped he could keep her safe from another attempt on her life.

When Liz walked into the inn, Sadie popped her head out of the quilt shop. She pointed a finger at Liz. "Material Girls meeting tonight at seven. Can you come?"

"I wouldn't miss it. I'll brew coffee and hot chocolate and bring them over." Liz reached down to pat Beans, lying prone on his rug. "Any news from Mary Ann?"

Sadie's face sagged, and for a moment she looked every inch of her seventy-plus years. "It's not good. But rather than have you hear it secondhand, I'll let her tell all of us tonight. That's the main reason for the meeting. We've got to support our Mary Ann."

Liz sucked in a breath. Her fears about Mary Ann being a suspect were valid. Then she squared her shoulders. Although she wasn't practicing law anymore, she could put her knowledge to use helping her friend. *And I will, every ounce of it.*

"That's right. We do. I'll see you a little later." Liz remembered she owed Naomi an update, and once she reached the front desk, she placed the call.

The inn's front door opened while Liz was saying good-bye to Naomi. Connie and Ron entered, both looking weary and woebegone.

"Hot coffee and cookies?" Liz offered. She wasn't in the mood for socializing, but she had to tuck away her problems and care for her guests.

"That sounds great," Connie said. "Wow, what a day."

"Thanks, Liz." Ron followed Connie into the sitting room, where they sat on a sofa together.

Liz hurried along to the kitchen, mentally deciding which cookies to pull out. An assortment might be nice. In the end, she included some of Sarah's raisin cookies along with molasses and chocolate chip cookies. She'd spend a few moments with her guests and then reheat some soup for dinner. She wasn't hungry, but she knew she needed to eat something.

The couple was uncharacteristically silent as Liz entered the room with the tray. She placed it on the coffee table. "Help yourself. Shall I start a fire?"

"Please," Connie said with a shudder. "It's not very cold out today, but I feel chilled inside."

I can relate to that. As Liz built a fire, she covertly watched the couple out of the corner of her eye. They seemed entirely normal as they sat and sipped, chatting lightly about this and that. But she knew from her experience that criminals were often adept at covering their misdeeds. Lying often went with the package as did proclamations of innocence. Sometimes she wondered if they really believed their own lies, an effort to hide the truth, even from themselves.

Once the fire was crackling satisfactorily, Liz poured herself a cup of coffee and sank into a chair, a sigh escaping.

"My thoughts exactly," Ron said.

"I'm so thankful Claudia is going to pull through." Connie's eyes glittered in the firelight. "I hope she'll be out of the hospital by Thanksgiving."

"I hope so too," Liz said. "Speaking of Thanksgiving, are you still planning to stay? I understand if you want to leave."

Ron and Connie exchanged glances.

"I think we'll stay," Ron said. "We're hoping the kids will show up."

"Plus, I want to be around for Claudia." Connie bit her lip, blinking back tears. "She really needs people who care right now."

Ron patted his wife's knee. "I'm proud of you. I know you've had your differences with Claudia, but I'm glad to see you've put them aside."

Connie took her husband's hand. "What are friends for?"

A little later as Liz carried carafes into Sew Welcome, she reflected on Connie's words. *Friends are there to support each other, no matter what*, she thought. *And what would we do without them?*

Most of the Material Girls—Sadie, Opal, Naomi, and Caitlyn—were already gathered in the workroom, occupied with the latest group project, quilts for premature babies.

To a chorus of greetings, Liz set the hot drinks on a table next to a tray of mini cheesecakes. "Naomi, did you make these? They look scrumptious."

"I did indeed. I thought we needed something special tonight, even if Thanksgiving is in a few days." Naomi set aside her stitching.

Everyone rose and joined Liz at the table for refreshments.

"I'm not even going to try to diet this week," Caitlyn said, "but I'm scheduling extra exercise sessions."

"Wait until you hit middle age," Sadie warned, "and a fast metabolism is a distant memory. Exercise or not."

Thankful that working around the inn kept her reasonably fit, Liz poured a cup of hot chocolate and selected raspberry and lemon cheesecake bites. "Is Mary Ann coming?"

Opal peered out the window. "I think I see her pulling in now."

They took their seats again, and a moment later, Mary Ann entered, brushing her silvery bob into place. She dropped her bag and removed her tan trench coat. "Hello, everyone." Spotting the coffee, she beelined to the table. "Just what I need."

"How are you holding up?" Sadie asked her.

Mary Ann sat down between Liz and Opal. "Not good." Liz had never seen the normally serene Mary Ann so tense and unhappy. Frown lines creased her forehead and bracketed her mouth. "I have never been interrogated by the police, and I hope I never have that pleasure again."

Sadie gave Mary Ann a hug. "Relax first before you fill us in."

While Mary Ann sipped her coffee and nibbled on a peanut butter cheesecake bite, Liz told the group about her visit to the hospital and Claudia's expected recovery.

"I'm so glad." Opal clapped. "I prayed that she would be spared."

"From what I heard," Liz said, "the prompt medical treatment did the trick."

"We do have a good hospital," Caitlyn said. "Even if I do say so myself."

Someone's phone rang with a loud classical tone. "That's mine." Mary Ann scrabbled around in her handbag and answered. Everyone waited quietly while she spoke to the caller. "I'm sorry you feel that way, but I understand. Take care." She hung up, her lips pressed into a grim line. "There goes my last pie order. Except yours, Liz. All canceled. I guess bad news travels fast."

"People are canceling because of what happened to Claudia?" That thought hadn't even crossed Liz's mind. She had every intention of serving Mary Ann's pies on Thanksgiving.

"Yes. They're trying to be nice about it, but let's face it. Claudia collapsing after tasting my pie wasn't exactly a good advertisement." Mary Ann gave a strangled laugh that turned into tears.

Opal passed her a lace-trimmed handkerchief with a pat on the arm.

"That's rotten," Caitlyn said. "There's no proof you were responsible."

Mary Ann waved a helpless hand. "I know. But I've gathered that they suspect a fast-moving poison. And since Claudia didn't react until she ate mine, it's easy to blame me."

"We need to figure out who did it." This bold announcement from the normally quiet Opal took the rest of the group by surprise.

"I agree. Despite her good qualities, Claudia appears to be someone who provokes strong reactions." Liz got up and closed the door to the workroom, not wanting Connie or Ron to hear their conversation.

She relayed the argument between the old rivals that she'd overheard in the bathroom at the football game.

"You think one of your guests might be involved?" Naomi asked. "That's creepy."

Liz drained her hot chocolate and thought about getting a refill. "I hope not, but there is obviously a long history between them."

"Don't forget Bob Stevens," Naomi said darkly. "Don't they always suspect the husband or wife? Or in this case, the ex-husband."

"He's obviously not over her," Caitlyn said. "Remember how he acted when she had that accident? He chased the ambulance to the hospital."

"Why did he show up at the scene anyway? I thought that was strange. Was he following her?" Sadie asked, then paused. "But Bob didn't go into the kitchen at the pie contest, did he?" She punched the air. "Darn it. There goes that theory."

"Maybe he was working with a partner," Naomi suggested. "The perfect crime. Get someone else to do it."

"And throw the blame on an innocent person along the way." The pieces fell into place in Liz's mind. "No matter whose pie it was, the plan would have worked, and the killers would be off scot-free. It *was* a perfect crime."

"Except Claudia didn't die," Sadie said with satisfaction. "You know what they say about the best-laid plans."

A rapping sounded on the shop door.

"We're closed," Sadie yelled. Then she got to her feet with a grumble. "I'd better go see who it is."

"Good idea. We can't afford to turn away any business right now." Mary Ann groaned and put her head in both hands. "I hope being under suspicion doesn't affect the shop too."

"You'll probably get more customers coming in," Caitlyn said. "You know how bloodthirsty and nosy people can be."

"Thanks. That really helps." Mary Ann's tone was dry, but a glimmer of her usual humor flickered in her eyes.

They heard Sadie unlocking the shop door, and then Sadie appeared in the doorway with Chief Houghton. "I had to let this guy in. He insisted."

"Sorry to interrupt your soiree," the chief said. "I went by your house, Mary Ann, and figured you were probably here. I need to talk to you for a minute."

Gasps and outcries of dismay flew around the circle.

He put up a hand in response. "I just want to talk, promise."

Mary Ann started to rise, but Opal reached over and put a detaining hand on her arm. "You aren't going anywhere. Chief, with all due respect, if you have something to say to Mary Ann, you can say it to all of us." The older woman fixed the chief with a glare that could melt ice.

Chief Houghton rocked back and forth on his heels, hitched up his belt, and scratched his head. "It's up to you, Mary Ann. We can talk here if you want."

Mary Ann sank back into her chair. "It's fine with me." She folded her hands in her lap and hunched her shoulders.

Before the chief could say anything, Liz asked, "Do you know what type of poison it was? And have you tested all the pies yet?"

"The answer to both questions is, not yet. The results aren't in."

"So you don't know for sure that Mary Ann's pie was poisoned," Naomi said.

The chief sighed. "No, we don't. But I'm asking you not to leave town for the next few days, Mary Ann."

"Are you aware that Thanksgiving is in three days?" Sadie said sharply. "She has plans to go see her children and grandchildren, right, Mary Ann?"

"That's right I do . . . but if . . ." Mary Ann began to wring her hands.

"Can they come to her house?" Sadie demanded. "Or is that forbidden too?"

The chief made an exasperated sound. "Of course she can have guests. I just want to be able to get ahold of her. It's protocol."

"Get ahold of her for what?" Opal took up the flag. "To arrest her for attempted murder?" She snorted, a rude sound that made her friends stare in surprise. "Ridiculous. Mary Ann Berne is not a cold-blooded killer."

Houghton's face reddened. "I'm not saying she is, but I've got to act prudently until all the evidence is in."

"What motive does she have?" Caitlyn barked. "Can you tell me that?"

The chief ducked his head, looking like he regretted the decision to enter the lioness's den. "We can't get hung up on motive. We have to look at means and opportunity. You know how many murderers don't seem to have a motive? Or one that might seem laughable or minor to a rational person?"

Sadie made a sound like a teakettle coming to a boil.

Seeing that the situation was deteriorating fast, Liz stepped in. "Chief, we understand you're just trying to do your job, and right now it's a very difficult one. We'll make sure Mary Ann stays in town. And you'll make sure she's not wrongly charged, right?"

"Of course." Chief Houghton sounded relieved. "This is a tough situation, and I appreciate your cooperation." He nodded. "Good night, ladies."

Liz showed him out and locked the door again.

When she returned, Sadie spoke up. "He thinks it's tough? He should be Mary Ann right now."

"He's only doing his job," Mary Ann said. "Don't blame him. He's not the one who laced my pie with poison."

"It might not have been your pie," Caitlyn said. "There were three others that she tasted before yours."

Mary Ann sighed, a deep, gut-wrenching sigh that heaved her chest. "Something's telling me it was mine."

"But you're innocent." Opal nodded firmly. "I'm going to ask my husband to see what he can find out at the Order of the Otter Lodge. George is one of the top-ranking members. I used to belong to the ladies' group, but I stepped down due to other obligations."

"That's right. There's no law saying that we need to sit back and wait for the police." Sadie regarded each woman in turn. "Let's work together and help Mary Ann clear her name."

"I'm in," Caitlyn said. "Of course, I have to follow hospital policies about privacy, but I'll keep my ears and eyes open when I'm there."

Naomi also chimed in with support, vowing to keep her ear to the ground for local gossip at the bakery.

"I'll keep an eye on the Greggs," Liz said. "They also know Bob Stevens pretty well, so maybe I can learn more about him on this end."

Mary Ann's eyes filled with tears. "You're all wonderful. How can I ever thank you?" She got up and went around the room, giving each woman a big hug.

"Don't worry about it." The normally gruff Sadie blinked back tears of her own as she patted Mary Ann on the back. "You'd do the same for us."

"You bet I would." Mary Ann's reply was fervent. "But let's pray I never have to."

Amen to that. Liz headed for the table to gather the empty carafes. It'd been a very long, hard day, and she was eager to go to bed.

Liz was banking the fire in the sitting room when the front door opened, and Piper and Tony came in.

Tony threw himself into a recliner and put up the footrest. "Guess what, Liz? Our segment is canceled."

"That's too bad." The food show feature was another casualty of the poisoning incident. She and many others in town had been looking forward to the publicity generated by the pie contest.

Piper sank down onto the sofa. "The whole thing is a disaster—for Claudia most of all, of course. Have you heard anything, Liz?"

"When I was at the hospital earlier, the doctor said she would recover." Liz set the poker back in the stand. "So that's good news."

"Can you believe it? Our sweet little cooking segment turned into a crime show." Tony sounded disgusted. "I guess I'll be leaving for Chicago early."

"Leave the footage," Piper said. "Maybe I can salvage some clips for another feature."

The footrest clunked down. "You're not going to take that offer?"

What offer? Liz held her tongue despite her curiosity.

Piper's cheeks flushed. "Of course not. The video belongs to the network. I'm not going to sell it to that tabloid show." She glared at her cameraman. "I thought you knew me better than that."

"Sorry. I was out of line." Tony frowned as he studied his boss. "I can't figure out why you would want to hang around here instead of going back to LA."

"I need a break." Piper ducked her head, her hair swinging to hide her face. "I'll be back after the holiday."

A note of strain in Piper's voice told Liz she was lying. *What is going on? Why is Piper going to stay?* The vague suspicions Liz had harbored about the television host hardened into certainty.

As soon as Tony went upstairs, Liz said, "You have relatives here in Pleasant Creek, don't you, Piper?"

11

Piper burst into tears. "How did you guess?"

Liz brought a box of tissues over and set it on the table beside her guest, then perched on the sofa. "I put two and two together. You see, my mother was Amish, and that's why I moved to Pleasant Creek. I wanted to connect with my roots. I think I recognized that same longing for family in you." Now Piper's questioning Sarah made sense. She'd been seeking news of her family.

Piper scrubbed at her face and eyes with a tissue. "Does your mother live here?"

"No, she passed away. I didn't find out about her background until I read her diary after her death. She moved away and changed her identity."

"That's what I did." Piper balled up the tissue in her hand. "I ran away to Hollywood, picked a new name, and went to college. I had a passion for the performing arts, and you know the Amish don't exactly embrace those."

"My mother's case was a little different," Liz said. "She had trouble with someone in the community. But that's all over now, and I'm building relationships with her extended family."

Piper took a deep breath. "I used to be Martha Mast."

"And Elmo is your father," Liz said softly. "I heard that he is ill."

Worse than that, he may not make it. Liz didn't want to be the one to share the devastating news.

"Yes, he is." Tears threatened again. "That's one reason why I pushed so hard to do the segment here. It gave me an excuse to come back to Pleasant Creek and find out what was going on." She dabbed at her eyes. "A friend outside the Amish community said he was sick, but she didn't know any details."

"Did you take your baptismal vows?" Liz knew that was the threshold for how family members would regard someone who left. Cutting ties with the church after taking vows was much more serious than beforehand.

"No, I didn't. But my parents were very angry at my decision to pursue film studies. They had strong ideas about how I should live my life, and I didn't agree with them. It was easier to just leave." She hiccuped. "But now I regret it."

Liz had an idea. "I ordered a turkey from your father's farm, and I have to go pick it up tomorrow afternoon. Why don't you come with me?"

Piper shrank back against the sofa cushions. "You think I should?"

"I do. I wouldn't be surprised if this health crisis has softened their hearts too." Liz reached over and squeezed Piper's hand. "It's worth a try."

"I don't know. What if . . . ?" Her voice trailed off.

"How about this? Sleep on it and let me know tomorrow. No pressure." Sensing Piper needed to be alone, Liz rose. "I'm going to get ready for bed. Stay up as long as you like."

———————————

Too early the next morning, a ringing telephone woke Liz. She reached for the bedside extension, her heart pounding. *Was Steve—?*

"I'm sorry to bother you at this hour," Mary Ann said, "but the police are here, and they've got a search warrant."

Liz sat up in bed, pushing back the covers. She fished for her slippers. "What for?"

"They didn't say. But they're crawling all over my house and yard." Liz heard a muffled sob.

"I'll be right there. See you in a few." Liz hung up and ran for the bathroom. Although she hadn't practiced criminal law, she knew the ins and outs. Having your property searched by the police was an unnerving experience, even if you were innocent.

None of the guests were up yet, so Liz put on coffee and left a note for Sarah to set out muffins, bagels, and fruit when she arrived. Then she zoomed over to Mary Ann's quiet neighborhood and her attractive white frame house. Sadie's pink Jeep was parked in the driveway, along with several police cruisers.

Liz knocked on the front door and entered, not waiting for anyone to answer. Mary Ann was huddled on the stairs to the second floor, Sadie hovering beside her. Liz glimpsed officers in the kitchen and living room, visible through archways. Doors and cabinets were opened and slammed shut as they searched.

"I'm so glad you're here, Liz." Mary Ann's smile was grateful.

"This is an outrage." Sadie stood in a wide-legged stance, her arms crossed. "The chief didn't say a thing about this last night."

"He couldn't," Liz said. "If he'd warned Mary Ann, she could have gotten rid of any evidence."

Sadie harrumphed. "I suppose so. But there isn't any evidence. It's just a shot in the dark."

"Ms. Eckardt, good morning." The chief came through the archway to the kitchen.

"Good morning, Chief. This is quite a surprise." Liz cocked a brow.

He glanced around, his eyes not meeting hers. "Uh, yes. Some results came in, so we're taking a look."

"Results?" Liz gave him her best lawyer stare. "I hope you're looking at other people in the contest. You know Mary Ann didn't do this."

"I can't say any more." Houghton nodded at Mary Ann. "I suggest you get an attorney."

Mary Ann groaned.

Sadie moved closer and patted her on the back. "Remember, Mary Ann, innocent until proven guilty."

"You found something in the tests then." Liz's words weren't a question.

Again the chief avoided eye contact. "I'm not allowed to share that right now. Mary Ann's attorney will need to contact us. If she can't afford one, then we'll appoint a public defender if she is arrested." At Mary Ann's cry, he added, "We haven't issued an arrest warrant, but I think it's wise to seek counsel."

"No public defender for you, my girl," Sadie said. "Liz, can you help us find someone?"

"I don't really know anyone local . . ." Liz thought about her criminal law contacts in Boston. "But I do know someone who can help me." She stepped outside and made a call, grateful that her friend was an early riser. He suggested Nina Davis in Blaketown. Liz checked her out online and discovered she had an excellent reputation and was active in the state bar association.

Nina was also an early riser, and she returned Liz's call immediately. "Let's meet at my office in two hours," she said, her tone brisk and efficient. She gave Liz the address.

Liz stepped back inside. "We're all set. Nina Davis is going to take your case. So as soon as the police are done here, let's head to Blaketown."

Mary Ann and Sadie rode with Liz, the business partners having made arrangements for Caitlyn to fill in at the shop for the morning.

The trio was silent during the short ride through the countryside to the nearby town. Farms were tucked among rolling hills adorned with trees wearing their autumn colors. The landscape's peace conveyed an attitude of rest in preparation for the winter ahead. Liz prayed the situation would soon resolve favorably for her friend, who also deserved a season of rest. The trip appeared to relax the travelers, and the atmosphere in the car lightened.

"The children and grandchildren are coming to my house," Mary Ann said, breaking the silence as they approached the outskirts of Blaketown. "They told me they're cooking." She chuckled. "The first time ever."

"It's about time," Sadie said. "I told my brother it was his turn. So we're doing a deep-fried turkey. He just bought one of those outdoor gas fryers."

"I've never had fried turkey," Liz said. It sounded greasy and awful to her.

"Oh, it's good," Sadie said. "The juiciest meat you'll ever eat."

"I'll take your word for it." Liz threw a smile at Mary Ann, who returned it.

"I'll give you both a plate of leftovers." Sadie was oblivious to their disinterest. "You'll probably want to buy fryers of your own."

Never in a million years. "Maybe so." Liz peered at a street sign and then at her GPS on the dash, which intoned, "Turn left here." After stopping for a passing car, she took a side road leading them off Blaketown's main street.

The attorney's office was one of a line of elegant older brick houses, now mostly occupied by businesses and organizations. A huge spider plant hung in the bow window of Nina's office.

"This is it." Liz turned into the small drive and parked at the rear.

Mary Ann clutched Liz's arm. "I'm nervous."

"Don't be," Liz said. "You know how they call attorneys 'advocates'? She's someone who is going to be looking out for your best interests and fighting for you."

"Like us," Sadie said, opening the rear door. "Only we don't have any clout in court."

Nina Davis perfectly fit the impression Liz had gotten over the phone. Petite with short, dark hair, she was a ball of energy and efficiency. Within ten minutes of being ushered into her office, she had the whole story and timeline written down in her notes.

"Once you delivered the pies, you didn't have access to the kitchen?" Nina asked Mary Ann. "You didn't go in there to tweak your pie or get a glass of water or anything?"

"None of us did. In fact, we didn't know until round one was over that Claudia was going to eat our entries."

"Hmm. And the first round of pies was fine." Nina swiveled in her chair, staring at the spider plant as she thought. She turned back around, tapped her pen on the desk, and picked up the phone. She made a couple of calls, introducing herself as Mary Ann's representation, and within a few minutes, the printer beside her desk was burping out sheets. "I'm having them send over the toxicology results," Nina told them.

Nina gathered the sheets and scanned them. "All right. They believe Claudia was poisoned with strychnine." At their confused looks, she added, "Rat poison, basically."

"Rat poison?" Mary Ann's face darkened. "Oh no. I have some of that in my shed. Do you think they found it?" She put both hands to her cheeks. "Of course they did."

"Almost everyone has rat poison around," Sadie said. "I have it out in the barn. That's not proof you did it."

Liz had a thought. "Did they find out which part of the pie was poisoned?"

A brief look of confusion passed over Nina's face. "I get it." She glanced at the report. "It was in the whipped cream."

"That's good news," Liz said. "Really good news."

"What do you mean?" Mary Ann asked.

"Whoever poisoned Claudia probably sprinkled the poison on the cream," Liz said. "It's white, isn't it? If it was in the filling, then you would have had to add it while it was baking. Anyone could have doctored the whipped cream."

"Anyone who went into the kitchen," Nina said. "And my client wasn't in there." She quirked a brow. "You didn't leave your pies unattended anywhere else, did you?"

Mary Ann shook her head. "In the morning I added the whipped cream and packed the pies up for the contest. I drove straight to the lodge and handed them over."

"That was a long shot, but I had to check." The phone rang, and Nina glanced at the incoming number. "I'd better take this." The attorney didn't say much, but when she hung up her expression was grim. "They've issued a warrant for your arrest, Mary Ann."

12

Mary Ann wailed at the news. "I can't believe this is happening. It's a nightmare."

"She's innocent," Sadie said. "How can they arrest her?"

Nina pursed her lips. "Apparently, they found rat poison in your shed, Mary Ann. And since it matches the toxicology reports, they feel they have enough to arrest you." She patted the desk. "But don't worry. I'll have you out on bail this afternoon."

"And we're going to find out who really did it," Liz said.

Nina cocked her head. "Come again?"

"Liz has been instrumental in solving a number of cases in Pleasant Creek. With our help," Sadie explained. "But we don't interfere with the police's investigation, of course." She provided a brief rundown of mysteries Liz and the Material Girls had worked on.

The attorney picked up her pen and twirled it in her fingers, swiveling back and forth in her chair. "Interesting. In many felony cases, we hire private investigators. Maybe in this case you can all serve that function."

"This is what we know so far." Liz gave Nina a summary of Claudia's relationships, mentioning her unusual divorce settlement and the disagreement with Connie.

"She doesn't even get along with our mayor," Sadie said. Glancing at Liz, she added, "Not that we suspect Jackson Cross, although he was at the contest."

"And don't forget the way Stevens' Motors is cheating people." Mary Ann's cheeks flamed. "They did $500 of unauthorized work on my car. Who knows how many others they've done that to."

"Caitlyn was having trouble with a car loan through them too," Liz put in.

"That's new since Kevin came on board, right, Mary Ann?" Sadie snorted. "Why wasn't *he* the target?"

Nina, busy scribbling notes, looked up with an amused smile. "Quite a lot of drama for a small town. Seriously, though, if this case makes it to court, you're giving me plenty to create doubt. That's all we have to do."

"We don't want to just get her off; we want to clear her entirely." Sadie's face was pinched. "Mary Ann has lived in Pleasant Creek her entire life, and it's not fair that her reputation and all her good work are going down the tubes."

"Having such good friends speaks well of your character, Mary Ann," Nina said softly. "I'm going to work hard to get these charges dropped."

Liz and Sadie accompanied Mary Ann to the police station, where they waited while she was booked. Then they followed her and Nina to court, where, fortunately, a judge held a bail hearing immediately. Due to her standing in the community and longtime residence, bail was granted. She was also warned to stay away from Claudia and not to contact her in any way.

Outside the courthouse, Nina promised to stay in touch and went off to another meeting.

After she strode away, Sadie said, "You're taking the rest of the week off, Mary Ann. I'll figure out how to cover the store."

"Are you sure? I know it's busy right now . . ." Mary Ann's whole body sagged with exhaustion.

"Yes, I'm sure. Call your kids and have them come over early. Take a break and relax."

"Relax? I'm not very good at that." Then she smiled. "But I am good at baking pies. And I'm not going to let this horrible situation spoil that for me. Liz, I'll be working on yours."

"Are you sure?" Liz was willing to make one or two herself if need be.

"Yes, I am. I want to do it." Mary Ann's mouth turned down. "But I think I'll skip the pumpkin for now."

"That's fine. I don't have much appetite for it myself at the moment." How long would it be before the image of Claudia biting into a gorgeous pumpkin pie and falling ill would be erased from her mind? Maybe when the real culprit was found.

Liz dropped off Mary Ann and Sadie at Mary Ann's, where Sadie had left her Jeep, and headed for the inn. Heartsick, she reviewed the day's events, from the search warrant to the bail hearing. Chief Houghton hadn't wasted any time securing Mary Ann's arrest.

According to the court documents, the police had found open containers of rat poison in Mary Ann's shed. Those combined with the tainted whipped cream on Mary Ann's pie led the district attorney to believe a case could be made. Like Sadie had said, almost everyone had that type of poison around. *How smart of the poisoner to use it. And how brilliant to use someone else's concoction as a delivery vehicle.*

As Liz entered the inn, Tony came down the stairs carrying his duffel bag. "Are you off to Chicago?"

He grinned, his fading black eye giving him a rakish air. "I am. By the way, I moved the camera equipment to Piper's room. She's going to take care of it."

"That's fine." Liz printed Tony a copy of the bill, which had been paid by the production company. "Come back and see us sometime."

"I'd like to. Pleasant Creek is a great little town." Tony folded the bill and tucked it into a side pocket of his bag. "And between you and me, I wouldn't mind seeing Caitlyn again."

Liz chuckled. "I'm sure she would like that."

Tony looked thoughtful, seemed about to say something, then shook his head. "I'll be off. Have a great Thanksgiving. Thanks for the hospitality."

"You're welcome. Take care."

The front door shut behind him, and Liz continued on her way to the kitchen. She was starving, and after lunch, she needed to go out to the turkey farm. *Piper's family's farm.* In the kitchen, she found Sarah removing a pan of molasses cookies from the oven.

Liz stopped short. "Sarah, I thought you'd be gone by now."

The Amish woman shrugged. "I thought I would help since you were so busy with poor Mary Ann's trouble."

"You heard about that?" Liz went to the coffeemaker, where fresh coffee awaited. She could tell by its delectable odor. She poured a cup and went to the fridge for cream.

"Everyone in town has heard that Mary Ann has been arrested." Sarah picked up a spatula and moved the cookies to a waiting rack. "I think it's a travesty."

After doctoring her coffee, Liz rummaged in the fridge for a container of leftover pea soup and a square of corn bread. She'd heat them in the microwave for lunch. "I think so too, but some people already consider her guilty." Hands full, she shut the fridge door with her hip. "Everyone canceled their pie orders with her. Except me."

"That's terrible." Sarah wrinkled her pert nose. "But it's like that in a small town. People can rally behind you or they can condemn you, all in a heartbeat."

"Well put." Liz popped the container of soup into the microwave and pushed buttons.

Sarah selected another baking tray from the cabinet. "I heard you are joining us on Thanksgiving after all."

"I am. And I'm very excited about it." Liz opened a drawer and chose eating utensils. The microwave beeped, and she stirred the soup and closed the door again.

"We are cooking a thirty-pound turkey. Can you imagine such a thing?" Sarah scooped up a ball of cookie dough with a spoon and dropped it on the pan.

"Wow. That's huge." Liz sat at the table with her soup. "After I eat, I'm going out to the Mast farm to pick up a turkey." She laughed. "It's nowhere near thirty pounds." She would never be able to wrestle a turkey that size into the oven.

"The Masts raise the best poultry around. That is where we got ours."

"That's what I heard. I think I ordered one of the last turkeys available." Liz was tempted to mention Piper's relationship to the family, but she held her tongue. It wasn't her story to tell. She did ask, "Is there any news about Elmo? I heard he's sick."

Sarah shook her head. "Nothing new as far as I know." She slid the filled pan into the oven and set the timer. "Do you want a cookie?" She smiled. "You really should try them before you serve them to your guests."

"I'd love a couple for the road." Liz breathed in the sweet, spicy aroma drifting from the oven. "I can already tell they're delicious."

With a sandwich bag of cookies in hand, Liz walked through the inn and found Piper in the sitting room reading a book. Liz entered the room. "I'm going to the turkey farm. And I've got treats." She shook the bag.

To her surprise, Piper set aside her book and rose. "I think I'll go with you." She grinned. "How can I resist fresh-baked molasses cookies?"

Despite Piper's joke, Liz could tell the other woman was nervous. Once they were in the car, Piper sat tensely in the passenger seat and stared at the passing scenery. Liz gave her her privacy by remaining silent and focusing on the drive.

As they drew closer to the farm, Piper sucked in a breath. "This is all so familiar . . . It's funny how you can remember every detail. Like that big tree on the corner and the neighbor's barn. I see they finally painted it." She pointed to a rolling, grassy field. "I used to play there with my brothers. I'd pick wildflower bouquets for my mother. Sometimes they'd wilt before I got home." She laughed at the memory.

"It must have been nice growing up in the country," Liz said. "Children here have much more freedom than in the city."

"True." Piper was silent for a moment. "Although my parents were strict and we had plenty of rules, it wasn't a bad life."

On that note, they reached the final stretch of road before the farm. Piper inhaled sharply and held her midsection. "My heart is pounding."

Liz reached out and squeezed Piper's arm. "I know exactly how you feel. I'll never forget my excitement and trepidation when I learned I had relatives here in town. I was so afraid they wouldn't accept me, since my mother had broken off contact when she left."

"But they did accept you?" Piper wore an expression of hopeful hunger.

"They did. In fact, I'm having Thanksgiving with my cousin Miriam's family." Liz felt a burst of joy every time she thought of her own happy ending in Pleasant Creek. *Please, Lord, give Piper a happy ending too!*

Liz slowed as they approached the farm, and Piper shifted in her seat, gazing around at the house and barns, the fields and turkey houses, sadly almost empty now. Liz thought of the hundreds of poor birds, their lives cut short for Thanksgiving meals.

Piper picked up on her thought. "I used to cry about the birds every Thanksgiving, but when dinner was served, I ate as much turkey as anyone else."

"I was just thinking that, seeing the empty cages." Liz pulled into the driveway. A few cars sat in the parking lot. Liz chose a spot on the end.

Piper shrank back, peering out at the young man Liz had seen on her last visit. He didn't look their way, intent on his destination of the barn. "I can't believe how big he's gotten. Micah, my brother's son. He was pretty young when I left."

"He's a thoughtful young man," Liz said. "He offered to take over the counter so Ezra could go into the house and sit with his father."

"My father—my Vater." Staring straight ahead, Piper blinked furiously, but tears rose and fell down her cheeks in shining rivulets.

Liz dug around in her purse and produced a packet of tissues. "Here you go." She handed Piper one.

"Sorry." Piper gave a light laugh as she dabbed at her eyes. "You must think I'm a basket case. All I've been doing since I got here is cry."

"Totally understandable." Liz watched as customers emerged from the barn, lugging paper sacks containing turkeys, she guessed. By mutual consent, they stayed in Liz's car until the last person drove away, their wheels crunching on the gravel.

"Ready to go in?" Liz put her hand on the door handle.

Piper hesitated, then inhaled visibly, releasing her breath in a sigh. "Yes, I am."

Liz led the way into the shop. "Hello, Ezra. I'm here for my turkey."

"Good afternoon." Ezra nodded politely. When he noticed the woman behind Liz, his mouth dropped open.

"Yes, Ezra, it's me. Martha." With a tremulous smile, Piper stepped forward. She turned to Micah. "I'm your aunt, but you probably don't remember me."

The young man glanced at his father, then back at Piper, confusion flitting over his handsome features. "I think I might . . . You used to read to me before bed."

"That's right. I did. You've turned into a fine young man."

Micah's cheeks flushed, and he looked down. "Thank you."

"Why are you here?" Ezra's tone was low and filled with suppressed anger. "You left us, remember?"

Piper bit her lip. "I know. But not a day has gone by that I haven't thought of you all."

"It was your choice, Sister. Don't forget that." He curled his lip, his fists clenched at his sides.

13

Liz's belly twisted in sympathy for Piper, who appeared stunned by her brother's hostility. After a moment, Piper turned and fumbled for the doorknob. "This was a mistake . . ."

"Vater, are you really going to do this?" Micah asked. His jaw worked in distress. "She is still family, and you said family is the most important thing of all."

Ezra considered his son's words, his brows knitted in a scowl.

Piper twisted the knob and pulled, jerking the door open.

Before she could slip out, Ezra spoke again. "Wait . . . wait, Martha." He came around the counter and followed his sister, who was still attempting to get out of the building. He took her shoulder gently and turned her to face him. "Forgive me? I am glad you are home," he said simply.

"Of course I forgive you." Piper threw herself into his arms, and they embraced, Piper crying on Ezra's white linen shirtfront. Finally, she pulled away, smiling, wiping her eyes on her sleeves. "I must look a mess." She laughed.

"You look beautiful to me." Plucking at his beard, he asked, "Do you want to see Vater? He . . . he isn't doing well. Although better than the doctor predicted, thank *Gött*."

"I heard he was ill. And, yes, I want to see him." Piper took a deep, shuddering breath and straightened her clothing. "I must see him."

"I can come back and get you later, Piper," Liz said. "If you'd like to stay awhile."

Piper faced Ezra. "What do you think? Would that be okay?"

"You could stay for supper," Ezra suggested. "That will give us time to catch up." A smile played around his mouth. "I have several other children you have not met yet."

Piper squealed, clapping. "I'd love to. I can't wait to see them."

Liz agreed to come back at eight p.m., and after retrieving the turkey from Micah, she headed for her car. As she opened the door to the backseat, where she placed the turkey, she glanced toward the farmhouse, imagining the reunion inside.

Warm satisfaction glowed at her small part in bringing Piper and her family together. The Masts would have a wonderful Thanksgiving indeed.

The next morning Piper wandered into the kitchen as Liz was taking a pan of apple crumb coffee cake out of the oven. "That smells fabulous," she said, yawning.

"It will be ready in a few minutes." Liz set the pan on the counter to cool. "Help yourself to coffee."

As Piper slouched toward the coffee, Liz stole a glance at her guest. Despite being half-awake, Piper had a much lighter demeanor, a quiet joy that shone in her eyes. "Did you sleep well?"

Piper poured cream into her coffee. "I sure did." She glanced up at Liz. "Thanks again for taking me out there. I'm so happy. I feel like I'm walking on air." She leaned against the counter and took a sip of the hot brew.

Liz pulled a bowl of fruit salad out of the fridge. "I'm really glad. I assume you're spending Thanksgiving with your family?"

"My *family*." Piper grinned. "Yes, I am. I still want to keep the room. In fact, I want to extend the booking for another week. I hope that's not a problem."

Liz reviewed her upcoming reservations. The Sunset Room was open. "No, that will be fine. I'm glad to have you stay as long as you want."

"Great. I'll help you carry something." Piper put her mug down and picked up the fruit salad.

Liz brought the coffee cake into the dining room and then returned to the kitchen to make a big pan of scrambled eggs with cheese and ham. Connie and Ron entered the dining room just as she set the platter of eggs on the table.

"Good morning," Ron said, rubbing his hands together. "I see our timing is perfect."

Liz arranged the serving spoon on the platter. "Yes, it certainly is. Did you sleep well?"

"Like a top." Ron held a chair out for his wife, then sat. "What does that expression mean anyway?"

"I'm not sure," Liz said. "But that's true of many common sayings, isn't it? You two want coffee?"

They nodded.

Connie and Piper began chatting about Piper's family reunion news while Liz fetched coffee and juice.

"What are your plans for today?" Liz asked Ron when she set mugs and a carafe on the table.

"I think we're going to poke around the shops. The celebration is hosting a children's game day at the school, and that's not really our cup of tea."

"There's a concert tonight at the school too," Connie said. "An orchestra and chorus."

Liz's cell phone pealed in the kitchen, and she excused herself to answer, wondering if it was Mary Ann. To her surprise, it was Jackson.

After they exchanged pleasantries, he asked, "Would you like to go out to dinner at Mama's Home Cooking and then to the concert at the school? I've heard it's going to be outstanding. Excellent musicians and singers."

Liz laughed in delight. "We were just talking about that. The concert, I mean. I'd love to."

A few minutes later, they hung up and Liz caught herself smiling. It was fun having an outing with a good friend to look forward to. Her daily chores, although she enjoyed them, would be that much more pleasurable.

The rest of the day was quiet and fairly uneventful. Sarah was off, so Liz took care of the two bedrooms and baths, and then tidied the main floor. She double-checked her recipes for the next day and discovered a missing ingredient that required braving the madhouse of the grocery store to pick it up. But, actually, she enjoyed the hustle and bustle, the holiday excitement in the air. She threw a couple of bills in the charity bucket outside the store, glad she could be of help, no matter how small.

Her last stop was at Mary Ann's to pick up the pies she had ordered. Two cars Liz didn't recognize were in the drive, and when she rang the bell, she heard running footsteps and children's voices.

The door opened to reveal a small boy. "Who are you?" he asked.

A little girl jostled him out of the way. "Let me answer the door."

"Who's at the door? Oh, Liz, hi. Come on in." Mary Ann rushed down the hallway from the kitchen. "You remember Owen and Lillian."

Liz smiled at the cute youngsters. "Nice to see you again. Is it fun staying with your grandmother?"

The little girl tried to hide behind Mary Ann, but she said, "Yes, it is. We're having turkey tomorrow."

"Turkey!" Owen shouted and danced his way down the hall. "Turkey, turkey, turkey!"

"Indoor voice, Owen," a woman called from the kitchen.

Owen quieted but raced away, circling back into the living room, where he hopped onto the sofa to join three other children watching television. Liz recognized Owen's brothers, Aiden and Caleb, and Lillian's sister, Mia.

In the kitchen, two attractive young couples—Mary Ann's children, Heath and Lauren, and their spouses, Charlotte and Gavin—were sitting around the kitchen table.

"I need to get over to the inn," Lauren said, swinging a bob like her mother's. "I usually visit the quilt shop when we're in town."

"Not this time. We're laying low." Gavin smiled at his wife. "You'll just have to watch football."

Lauren laughed and gave her husband a love tap on the shoulder. "Not in a million years." Her face sobered. "Seriously, though, this whole thing is ridiculous and awful. How can anyone think Mom . . . ?" She blinked and stared down at the table.

An uneasy silence descended on the kitchen.

Heath pushed back his chair with a muffled exclamation. He stalked to the coffeepot, where he poured himself a refill. "I can't stand it. I know we agreed not to talk about it until after Thanksgiving, but it's gnawing at me." He lifted the pot toward Liz, who shook her head.

His wife glanced toward the living room. "Keep your voice down, Heath." Charlotte turned to Liz and said, "We agreed to keep the news away from the kids. We didn't want to spoil their holiday."

"Sadie suggested I stay home this week." Mary Ann pinched her forehead. "She's afraid people might accost me."

Liz thought about the questions and comments people would have for Mary Ann if they ran into her or if she was working at the store. "She's right." She glanced around at the concerned faces. "Your mom has a great attorney, which is a good first step. In addition, we—Mary Ann's close friends—are not going to stand idly by. We're trying to find out who did this. No, not trying, we're *going* to find out." Inwardly, Liz quailed, hoping she could live up to her brave words.

Mary Ann gave Liz a grateful smile. "Since Liz moved to town, we've helped her solve a number of cases. She's a former attorney."

"Really? I'm so glad to hear that." Lauren's expression conveyed total faith in Liz.

Liz sent up a silent prayer that she would indeed bring the person who poisoned Claudia to justice. Mary Ann and her family were counting on her.

"What will it be?" Doris Henderson, the owner of Mama's Home Cooking, stood next to Liz and Jackson's booth with her notepad. She winked. "I recommend the meat loaf." The meat loaf dinner was the evening's special.

"I'll have that, please." Liz tucked the menu back into the holder.

"Make that two," Jackson said, following suit with his menu.

"Gravy on the mashed potatoes?"

Liz and Jackson exchanged looks. "Yes," they said in unison.

"It sure is busy in here tonight," Liz said. All the booths were full, the counter seats were taken, and the tables in the middle of the floor were packed with customers. A line waited by the door.

"We've been slammed all day," Doris said. "The chamber's promotion really worked. All kinds of people are in town. And it doesn't look like they're leaving even if Thanksgiving is tomorrow." She appeared poised to whirl away, then changed her mind, leaning over the booth and lowering her voice. "How's Mary Ann holding up?"

Liz shrugged. "About as well as can be expected."

"You tell her I'm rooting for her." Doris shook her head. "There's no way on God's green earth that she's guilty."

"I will," Liz said, heartened by this show of support.

"It sounds to me like the evidence is purely circumstantial," Jackson said after Doris left to put in their orders. They were in the last booth, but he took the precaution of speaking quietly to avoid being overheard by fellow diners. Liz had given him a brief overview of events to date on the way to the restaurant.

"I agree," Liz said. "A lot of people had access to the kitchen, and no one knew which pies were going to be chosen until after the first round."

"That narrows down the time frame for sure." Jackson took a sip of his soda. "I've tried to remember which people were going in and out. I did go into the kitchen once when the Otter ladies wanted me to carry out a coffee urn."

"Was anyone in there with you?"

Jackson shook his head. "I went in, got the urn, and left. The pies were all still in the walk-in cooler at that time."

Loud laughter at the counter caught Liz's attention. Every diner-style restaurant had its regulars, customers who liked to sit at the counter for hours to drink coffee and shoot the breeze. Mama's Home Cooking was no exception, and Liz saw that one of the regulars, an elderly man, was making a big deal out of choosing dessert from the pie slices in a case.

"How do I know that one of them ain't poisoned?" he said loudly. "You could have it in for me, Doris."

"That's right," his companion said. "You could pull a Mary Ann on us."

"Uh-oh," Jackson said. "This isn't good."

Others in the restaurant turned to watch, waiting for Doris's reply.

The plainspoken restaurant owner put both hands on her hips and said, "If I was going to do away with you, Jack, or you, Ernie, I would have done it years ago when you first got on my nerves."

Everyone in the place burst into laughter. Jack and Ernie hunched their shoulders and muttered. The rest of the customers turned back to their meals, and within a minute or two, the conversation level was back at full volume.

Sympathetic humiliation for her friend made Liz go hot and cold. Even if Mary Ann was cleared—and she would be, Liz assured herself—she might still face suspicion and taunts from people in town.

Jackson seemed to pick up on her thoughts. "Don't worry. When this is over, we'll broadcast the news." He reached across the table and squeezed her hand. "And I'll personally see to it that Jack and Ernie and others like them keep their mouths shut."

"Thanks. At times like this you learn who your friends really are." Liz smiled at the handsome mayor, glad she could count him among her supporters.

───────────── ///////////////////////// ─────────────

The school parking lot was packed with vehicles, and Jackson ended up parking on a nearby side street. "I'm sorry we have to walk," he said.

"No problem." Liz gestured at her boots. "These are very comfortable. Besides, after that meal, I need the exercise."

"I hear you. Doris really piles on the mashed potatoes."

They climbed out of the car, and before Jackson locked it, he searched his coat pocket for the tickets. "I'm always nervous I'm going to forget these." He found the cardboard stubs. "All set."

Other people joined them on the trek to the school auditorium, which was brightly lit and welcoming.

"I haven't been to an event here," Liz said. "Games in the gym, yes."

"Then you're in for a treat," Jackson said. "A benefactor donated the funds to add it onto the high school a few years ago."

A ticket taker relieved Jackson of his tickets, handed them programs, and directed them to their seats in the balcony.

"I hope you don't mind it up here," Jackson said. "I like it because I can see everything."

"It's fine," Liz reassured him.

They found their seats and pushed down the folded-up cushions to sit. Liz looked around. The dimly lit room was almost full, a tangible sense of anticipation in the air as the audience chatted softly. Red velvet curtains were drawn across the stage and framed the windows along the sides.

A few minutes later the houselights flickered, and then the curtains drew back to reveal the empty chairs of an orchestra. The audience broke into applause as the musicians entered and took their places, followed by the conductor.

The first piece, a horn-rich classical composition that evoked ancient banquet halls, immediately captured Liz's attention. She settled back to listen, allowing her thoughts to drift on a journey created by the music.

Partway through the first segment, a man and a woman edged along the row of seats, apologizing as they went.

Liz glanced over, noticing they were headed for two empty seats to her left. She shifted back in her seat and pulled her knees to the side to allow them to pass.

In the dim light, she first recognized Bob. Then she spotted his companion, and her heart lurched. Why was Bob here with her?

14

Tiffany smiled down at Liz. "Sorry," she squeaked, sidling past. She and Bob settled into their seats and turned their attention to the performance.

As for Liz, she had been jolted out of her enjoyment of the music. *Why shouldn't Bob date Tiffany? After all, he's single.* But all the logic in the world couldn't erase a niggling discomfort at seeing the duo together in light of Claudia's poisoning. Also odd was that, at the hospital, Tiffany had relied on Kevin to provide comfort instead of Bob, who had also been there.

Forcing her attention back to the orchestra, Liz tried to shove her speculations aside. Maybe the attraction was recent, sparked by mutual concern over Bob's ex-wife. Liz sighed. That didn't make sense either.

A spotlight came on, revealing a twelve-person chorus standing at one side of the stage. The conductor waved his baton, and an especially operatic soprano belted out a few high notes that sent chills down Liz's spine. With gratitude she allowed herself to be swept up into a soaring chorale piece backed by violins.

At intermission, the houselights came up.

Liz turned to Tiffany. "Are you enjoying the show?"

Tiffany shrugged. "It's okay. Classical music is more Bob's thing. Right, Bob?"

Bob leaned forward so he could see Liz, and to her alarm she noticed that his eyes were bloodshot and his face was drawn. *Is he ill or worried about something?*

"I like classical music. It kind of sweeps you away." He made a clumsy gesture with one hand, and his words were slow and deliberate.

Liz amended her evaluation to include heavy drinking. *I hope Tiffany is the designated driver.*

Jackson nodded a greeting at the couple. "Do you want to go down for refreshments?" he asked Liz.

"Sure. I'd love to stretch my legs." Liz pushed herself out of the engulfing seat and stood. "Nice to see you both," she said to Tiffany and Bob.

They called something after her as she left.

By the time Liz and Jackson returned from drinking lemonade in the lobby, the couple was gone, and they didn't come back for the second half of the concert.

———————————— *//////////////////////////* ————————————

Thanksgiving morning dawned raw and cold, the thick, gray clouds blocking the sun. Liz rose even earlier than usual, the preparation of the dinner foremost in her mind. There was still no word from the Greggs' offspring, but she planned to cook for six. She was sure someone would enjoy the leftovers.

Her first task was to switch on lights and build a fire, creating an oasis of cheer to push back the gloomy day. In the kitchen, she turned on the radio, tuned low to classical music, and brewed coffee and whipped up a batch of apple crumb muffins. Breakfast would be light today in anticipation of a one o'clock dinner.

Next, she cut up celery and onions and cubed the day-old bread. Parsley, sage, and thyme would flavor the traditional stuffing recipe passed down by her mother. The whole array—green bean casserole, sweet potato soufflé, whipped potatoes, whole-cranberry sauce, and of course, turkey and gravy—were classics from the family celebrations Liz remembered with such fondness.

Her plan had been to create a memorable meal for the Greggs. The thought of the forlorn couple eating alone stabbed her heart. *Please, Lord, let those children show up.*

She couldn't imagine it if Steve decided to cut her off. They had scheduled a call later, a tradition on holidays when he wasn't able to come home.

After the muffins were done, Liz slid the bread cubes into the oven to brown and sat down for a quick break. The streusel-style whole-grain muffin was crumbly sweet, spiced with cinnamon and nutmeg. It was the perfect thing to keep her going.

The doorbell rang while Liz was wrestling the stuffed turkey into the oven. The Greggs were sleeping late, so she quickly shut the oven door and hurried to answer, wiping her hands on her apron.

Three young women and a young man stood on the porch, fidgeting in the cold wind.

"Are Connie and Ron Gregg here?" one young woman asked. She had long, blonde hair streaming out from under a colorful knit cap. She wore a navy wool peacoat, as did the other blonde girl. The other pair—both dark-haired—wore leather jackets. All were dressed in jeans and boots.

A burst of warmth filled Liz's chest. *Hallelujah, Lord.* "Are you Brooke?"

"Yes, I am." A line appeared between the young woman's brows. "Is my mom here?"

"She is," Liz said, opening the door wide. She grinned. "I'm very glad to see you all. Somebody's got to eat the huge dinner I'm making."

"Did someone say dinner?" the young man asked. "I'm starving."

Brooke entered first, followed by the other blonde, who said, "Hi, I'm Taylor."

"And I'm Jessica." The brunette jerked a thumb at the only male. "That's my brother, Jake."

"Glad to meet you all. I'm Liz Eckardt, the innkeeper." She indicated the coatrack. "You can leave your coats here. If you're hungry, I'll set up breakfast in the dining room, but first you can warm up for a few minutes in the sitting room while I get your parents."

After herding them into the sitting room, Liz flew on winged feet to the second floor. She tapped on the door of the Heirloom Room. "Connie? Ron? Are you awake?"

She heard muttering voices, then shuffling footsteps.

Ron opened the door and peered out, hair standing on end. "Yes, Liz?"

"I've got a surprise for you both." Liz paused. "Your kids are here."

Ron pulled his head back, frowning. "Did you say—?"

A whoop sounded from deeper in the room, and Liz heard thundering feet. "They showed up?" Connie pushed past Ron, seemingly ready to run downstairs in her pajamas.

"Hon, hold on a second," Ron said. "They're here and not going anywhere. Let's get cleaned up and dressed."

Connie's face fell. "All right. But I'll be down in five. Or ten."

"Take your time. I'll get coffee and muffins for all of you." After going downstairs, Liz popped into the sitting room. "Your parents will be down shortly," she said.

"You mean my mom and stepdad," Taylor said, tossing her hair.

"No, she means my dad and stepmom." Jessica glared at Taylor.

Brooke looked distressed.

Jake sighed loudly. "Girls, I thought we settled all this. We're *family*."

Taylor broke into laughter. "That's right. We're family," she said in a thick accent, like a mob boss.

Jake picked up the joke. "And you'll take a long walk off a short pier in cement overshoes if you don't listen to me."

Brooke joined in. "And I'll—"

"I'll fetch coffee." Liz escaped to the kitchen, the sound of joking and laughter filling the sitting room.

Liz returned with a tray of coffee and muffins in time to witness the reunion.

Connie entered the room, followed closely by Ron. Connie stopped short, anxiety and hope in her eyes.

Brooke jumped up and ran to Connie's arms. "Mom, I'm so sorry."

Connie squeezed her tight. "It's all right, honey. I love you."

"I love you too." Brooke faced Ron. "I'm sorry. Welcome to our family." She gave him a hug. "I know you make Mom happy, and that's all that counts."

"Thanks, Brooke." Ron's voice thickened. "I'm glad to be here."

Taylor was next, and then Jake and Jessica hugged each parent in turn.

Liz put the tray down and backed out of the room. Breakfast could wait.

The phone rang as she entered the kitchen. It was Sadie. "Happy Thanksgiving, Liz."

"Same to you. I hope you have a great day with your family."

"You too. Listen, I wanted to give you an update. Claudia was released from the hospital last night."

"That's great news. I'm so glad." Liz tucked the phone on her shoulder and began to work on vegetable preparation for the main meal.

"Me too." Sadie gave a rueful chuckle. "Wouldn't want our friend to face murder one charges." She cleared her throat. "I also got an update from Opal."

"She talked to George?" Liz retrieved a bag of potatoes from the pantry.

"Yes. He asked the women who were at the lodge on the day of the contest to think about who was in the kitchen and when. Of course they're all upset, so who knows what they remember or how reliable it is."

"That's understandable. Stressful events tend to blank out your memory."

"They do indeed. Anyway, I wanted to keep you posted. Tomorrow we'll get back to work clearing Mary Ann."

"Sounds like a plan. Talk to you later." Liz hung up.

Then a terrible thought struck, causing her to fumble the potato she held. What if the killer tried again? Maybe her theory about the car accident was correct. The poisoning wasn't the first attempt but the second. She needed to find out what had happened to Claudia's wrecked car. She tamped down her frustration. The holiday meant she had to wait to get answers.

Setting speculation aside, she focused on her cooking tasks. Connie entered the kitchen as Liz was opening the oven door to check on the turkey, which was browning nicely.

"That smells fabulous," her guest said.

"Doesn't it? Roasting turkey is one of my favorite smells, along with coffee and bacon." Liz shut the oven door. "How can I help you?"

"We girls are content with fruit and yogurt for breakfast, but Ron and Jake want omelets if that's okay." Connie rolled her eyes. "Like father, like son." But her big smile revealed how much she was enjoying having her husband's children around.

Liz reviewed the fridge contents. "I'd be happy to whip up omelets. Ham and cheese with mushrooms sound okay?"

"Definitely." Connie clasped her hands together. "I am so, so happy the kids showed up. It's like a dream come true. And staying in your gorgeous inn is the perfect thing to help us bond."

"I'm really glad." At that moment, seeing the stars in Connie's eyes, Liz fervently hoped that she wasn't guilty of the attempted murder. That would certainly ruin the Gregg family's happy ending.

After breakfast was over, Liz went into her quarters and booted up the computer for a scheduled video call with Steve. She connected to the service and heaved a sigh of relief when she got the signal that he was connecting. Technology was wonderful—until it didn't work.

"Hey, Mom." Steve's smiling face filled the screen. "Happy Turkey Day."

A surge of love overflowed Liz's heart at the sight of her godson. "You too. Did they feed you well today?" Liz knew the armed services did their best to make holiday meals special for the enlisted men and women serving overseas, and it was already afternoon in Kosovo, so the midday meal would have been over.

"It wasn't too shabby. Not like home though." Steve's face fell briefly, but then he smiled again. "So what's happening in the big little town of Pleasant Creek?"

Liz didn't want to depress Steve with the bad news about Mary Ann and the poisoned pie contest, so she told him about her guests' family reunions instead.

"That sounds awesome. You're helping bring families together."

"Well, I'm not really doing it, but it seems to be working out that way right now." Actually, that was a good marketing idea—to advertise that the inn was available for family reunions. Small ones, of course.

"I can't wait to be there again. It's a great place." Steve went on to give her updates about his life in Kosovo, sharing anecdotes with his trademark good humor.

With reluctance, Liz said good-bye. "I've got to go work on dinner for my guests. But let's do this more often, okay?"

"Let's. Of course my schedule is so erratic . . . but I'll try, promise. Love you, Mom."

"Love you too." Blinking back tears, Liz signed off. The good news was that she had a wonderful son, and she thanked God for that blessing daily. The bad news was that he was thousands of miles away.

Preparing dinner absorbed Liz's attention for the next few hours. If she'd had more guests, she would have needed help, but for six, she could handle it just fine.

The stuffed turkey was a golden, juicy triumph, the mashed potatoes were whipped peaks of perfection, and the vegetables were colorful and tasty. For bread, Liz heated up fluffy, tender rolls from Naomi's bakery. Jewel-like cranberry sauce, a dish of olives, and a boat of gravy completed the meal.

The Gregg family dug in with abandon, and Liz had to exercise great restraint. She wanted to keep her appetite for dinner at Miriam's later that afternoon.

"Who wants pie?" Liz asked to groans around the table.

The women demurred, but Jake asked, "What kind do you have?"

"Pecan and apple," Liz said. "With whipped cream or vanilla ice cream."

Jake's mouth turned down. "Those sound great, but no pumpkin?"

Liz braced herself. Mary Ann had refused to bake another pumpkin pie right now, and she couldn't blame her. She had feared the question would come up since pumpkin pie and Thanksgiving were synonymous. *Why didn't the Pilgrims eat blueberry pie?*

Before she could speak, Connie piped up. "I think there's a town-wide moratorium on pumpkin pie this year." She paused dramatically. "A pillar of the community was poisoned by one earlier this week."

Taylor gasped, and Brooke said, brow creased, "Oh yeah, I think I saw something about that online. I didn't put two and two together, that it happened here."

"What was it, bad pumpkin?" Jessica looked puzzled. "I never heard of that."

"No, worse." Connie widened her eyes. "It was deliberate."

Oh, brother. Here we go. Liz cleared her throat. "Sorry to interrupt, but if you can tell me what you want, I'll get dessert for you. I've got to clean up before I head out to a family dinner." She put up a hand. "Not that I'm rushing you." *But I am nudging you along.*

"Sorry, Liz," Ron said. "I'll take pecan with whipped cream."

"I'll have a slice of both, with ice cream," Jake said. "Thanks."

"Coming right up. I'll brew a pot of coffee too." As Liz hurried out, she heard Connie go into full swing, sharing every lurid detail.

Despite the chilly day, the Greggs went out for a family walk after dessert while Liz cleaned up. She quickly loaded the dishwasher and stowed the leftovers, not bothering to clean off the turkey carcass yet. Her last task was to leave a note telling them to help themselves to leftovers if they wanted. She placed a fresh loaf of bread prominently on the counter for sandwiches.

On the drive out to Miriam's, light snowflakes began to fall. The fluffy flakes weren't sticking, so Liz enjoyed how pretty they looked swirling down over the fields and forests.

As usual, Liz's car was the only vehicle in the driveway since Amish families used horses and buggies. She always felt a little odd about that, but Miriam's warm welcome erased her lingering sense of being an outsider.

"Please come in, Liz. We are so happy to see you." Miriam's youngest daughters, Grace, who resembled Liz's mother, and Keturah, cute in pigtails, clustered around, greeting Liz with smiles and hugs.

Next Sarah hurried out to say hello. "Is everything all right at the inn? I am sorry I was not there today."

"Everything is fine. Guess what?" Liz said. "Connie and Ron's children showed up finally. So I had six at dinner. But it wasn't a problem."

"I am so glad for them," Sarah said. "Family should be together on holidays."

In the living room, Liz discovered not only Miriam's family gathered, but also the families of her aunt Ruth and uncle Amos. Now the thirty-pound turkey made sense. Liz said hello to everyone, then accepted a glass of cider and sat down to chat.

When it was time to eat, Liz helped the other women in the kitchen serve up big bowls of side dishes, baskets of bread, and condiments. The older girls set the table and carried out pitchers of cider and water. Isaac, Sarah's husband, lugged the giant turkey into the dining room.

After a silent prayer moment initiated by Miriam's husband, Philip, he picked up the carving knife and got to work. Bowls and platters of meat were passed around the table, everyone helping themselves.

Liz enjoyed the give-and-take, the multitude of voices at the table, as everyone enjoyed the meal. Even though many dishes were similar to what she had made, with the addition of turnip and squash, she was conscious that all the vegetables had been grown right here on the farm. The dinner was truly a celebration of the land's bounty.

"I am so glad you could join us," Miriam said, seated to Liz's right. "The day seems complete now."

Liz hugged her cousin. "Thank you for saying that. I feel the same way." Although Liz had loved celebrating Thanksgiving with her parents and friends, she relished being part of a large, multigenerational family gathering. The spectrum of life— from small children to elders—was represented.

When Liz took her leave later, the snow had stopped. But the colder evening temperature meant that some of it had stayed. The moonlit landscape was serene, and very few cars were on the roads.

Replete and content, Liz parked at the inn and climbed out of her car, eager to change for bed and relax with a cup of tea.

As she entered the foyer, Connie rushed out of the sitting room. "Liz, I'm so glad you're home. I didn't want to bother you at your relatives' house, but I'm terribly worried about Bob."

Because he's dating Tiffany? Hiding a smile she feared might be inappropriate, Liz set her purse down and unbuttoned her coat. "Why? What's wrong?"

Connie took a deep breath, placing one hand on her chest. "He was all alone today, even though we invited him to come over and join us for dinner."

Without asking me, but that's all right, I suppose. "Go on."

"I can't reach him on the phone. So I'd like to go over to his house and see if he's okay." Connie paused. "I wanted you to come with me." Then she answered Liz's unspoken question. "Ron isn't here. He went out with Jake to watch a game. And the girls are bonding over manicures, so I hate to disturb them."

Did she have a choice? Liz sighed and reached for her coat. "All right, I'll go with you. But he's probably sleeping in front of the television after eating turkey." *I'd like to be doing that myself.*

Liz was glad to learn that Bob lived in a town house only a few streets over. They reached the place within a few minutes, and Liz pulled up at the curb and parked at Connie's direction. The line of four homes appeared quiet and tucked in for the night, with only a few lights on here and there.

"He's in that unit." Connie pointed. "The second one from the right."

The blue light of a television flickered behind partially closed blinds, and Liz was certain her television and turkey theory was correct. But to appease Connie, she got out of the car and followed her to the front door.

Connie reached out to knock, and when her fist hit the door, it swung open. She glanced at Liz. "This is strange."

A shiver of alarm ran down Liz's spine. Although Pleasant Creek was a safe town, people didn't generally leave their doors open and unlocked, especially in cold weather.

"I think we'd better check on him," Liz said. She stepped into a small foyer, calling, "Bob? Bob, are you home?"

No answer.

Liz took another step. Through an archway, she glimpsed a man sitting in a recliner in front of the television. His head was bowed, his chin resting on his chest.

15

By the stillness of Bob's posture, Liz sensed something was wrong. "Bob?" She crept closer.

No answer. The television set droned on, the announcer giving game highlights.

"What's the matter with him?" Connie hovered in the doorway, a look of horror on her face.

"I don't know." Liz hurried to his side. Vomit stained the front of Bob's polo shirt and pooled in his lap. By its appearance, the accident had happened a while ago. She shook his shoulder gently. "Bob? Bob, can you hear me?" She reached for his wrist and felt for a pulse.

Nothing. Despite the heat of the room, his skin was cool.

Spots danced in front of her eyes, and she had to lean over and prop her hands on her knees. "Connie," she croaked. "Call 911. I think he's dead."

As Liz gathered air into her lungs she heard Connie's high-pitched tones in the background. Finally, she recovered enough to stand upright again and glance around. On the end table next to Bob was an almost empty bottle of whiskey and two glasses, one with an inch of amber liquid, the other holding a small amount of water. Scattered on the floor was an array of white pills.

Did Bob commit suicide?

Anguish twisted her heart at the thought. She didn't know Bob at all, but to be driven to such despair . . .

"They'll be right here." Connie's eyes were as big as saucers while she took in the scene. "Did he . . . kill himself?"

Despite that being her conclusion, Liz was reluctant to say it. Maybe the overdose had been accidental. Or he'd had a heart attack. "I think we'd better leave that for the coroner to determine."

On wobbly legs, Liz staggered into the foyer. "Let's wait outside." Connie seemed reluctant to leave the house, so she put her hand on the other woman's shoulder. "Let's go. The police won't like us contaminating their scene any more than we already have."

She pushed Connie through the front door onto the tiny porch, where they waited, shivering in the cold. The snow icing the ground and trees didn't look so festive anymore, its frosty sterility reminding Liz of the coldness of the grave.

"Can I call Ron?" Connie stood with hunched shoulders, her fists balled in her jacket pockets.

"How about waiting until the police get here?" Liz said. "The news will get out soon enough, but we need to let the chief deliver it to the family."

"Bob doesn't have any family." Connie's tone was abrupt. "Unless you count his ex-witch." She put a hand to her mouth. "Did I say that out loud? Sorry."

Liz took a subtle step away. While she needed to be polite to her guest, she had to admit the woman's erratic emotions and tactless comments were getting on her nerves. "Well, it'd be better for Claudia to learn it officially than on the street. Think about it."

Connie crammed her hands into her pockets again, swaying back and forth. "You're right."

Sirens sounded, and a moment later Liz saw the flicker of red and blue lights reflected in the treetops. A police cruiser and an ambulance raced around the corner onto Bob's street and stopped in front of his house. Lights came on in the adjacent units and across the street. Directly opposite, the front door opened, and an elderly man shuffled out onto the steps for a better look.

Chief Houghton emerged from the cruiser and trotted up the walk. "Where is he?"

"In the living room." Liz and Connie stood aside as the chief entered, followed shortly by two EMTs.

"Can we go now?" Connie asked Liz.

"No, I think we'd better wait. The chief is going to want to ask us some questions."

"How about we wait in the car? I'm freezing."

"Good idea." Liz's toes were blocks of ice. She led the way to the car, where they sat with the engine running.

After about ten minutes, the chief came outside, glanced around, and headed for Liz's car, walking around to the driver's side.

She rolled down the window. "How is he, Chief?" There wasn't much chance in her limited knowledge that Bob could be resuscitated, but you never knew.

Houghton shook his head, lips pressed in a grim line. He looked past Liz to Connie and nodded a greeting. "So, ladies, take me through this evening. Why did you come over here?"

Liz explained that Connie had asked her to check on Bob because he hadn't answered or returned Connie's call.

"Why was that such a concern?" Houghton asked Connie.

Connie shrugged. "He's been really down lately. We asked him to come over today so he wouldn't be alone on the holiday, but he said no. I gave him a call to check in with him. He always answers his phone. Or calls back right away." Her face crumpled. "I can't believe this."

"I know. It's really awful." Liz fished around in her bag for a tissue and handed it to Connie. "Chief, if there isn't anything else, can we go? I think Connie would like to see her husband."

The chief stood back. "Go on. I know where to reach you if I have any other questions."

As Liz drove away, she glanced at Chief Houghton in the rearview mirror; he watched them for a minute before turning toward the house. What a terrible thing to happen on Thanksgiving, being called out for an unexpected death. No doubt such things were the worst part of the chief's job.

On the way back to the inn, Connie called Ron, making him promise not to say anything to anyone at the sports bar where he and Jake were hanging out.

Liz tuned out the one-sided conversation, lost in her own thoughts as she navigated the familiar streets. Bob's death was definitely untimely and a tragedy. He was fairly young and seemingly healthy. Why had this happened? Maybe it was an unfortunate accident. She'd heard of people who mixed medications with alcohol and suffered adverse reactions.

But many suicides also used that method. Had Bob been that depressed? Had losing his wife and business driven him off the deep end?

Connie hung up as Liz pulled into the inn's driveway. "Ron will be right back. He's really upset."

"I don't blame him," Liz said, turning off the engine. "Bob was too young to die."

"I wonder who will get Bob's share of the business," Connie said, sliding her phone into her purse. She fumbled for the door handle.

"What do you mean?" Liz asked. "I thought Claudia got it all during the divorce."

Connie shook her head. "Not quite. Bob was still an owner, but he had no voting power. That was given to Kevin." She finally managed to open the door and slid out of the car.

Interesting. It must have been hard for Bob to stand by and watch another person run the company with his ex-wife. Liz opened her own door and got out, pausing to lock the car before following Connie into the inn.

Liz was definitely ready for that hot bath and a good book now. Otherwise, she'd be awake all night reliving the evening's disturbing experience. After making sure her guests were settled, she gratefully went to her quarters and locked the door.

The next morning, Liz bolted out of the kitchen the moment she heard Sadie's strident tones. "We're opening up in five minutes. Just give me a second and I'll let you in."

Liz found Sadie standing in front of Sew Welcome, juggling her belongings while unlocking the door. A pair of women stood nearby, eager to begin shopping.

That's right. It's Black Friday. Liz had always made a point of not participating in the annual ritual so fervently embraced by shoppers nationwide. She preferred to avoid the crowds and stay home. It wasn't her style to fight over the gifts of the moment. She preferred to thoughtfully build a list and take her time finding the perfect items.

Now Black Friday is coming to me. Or to my house, actually.

Sadie spotted Liz hovering. "Morning. Have a nice Thanksgiving?"

"I did. Thanks." Liz stood back to let the customers follow Sadie into the store. They headed for colorful bolts of cotton, and Liz and Sadie went to the checkout counter.

"Mine was great too. Relaxing." Sadie stowed her things behind the counter. "Caitlyn has a day off from the hospital, so she's coming in to help, thank goodness. I just know we'll be slammed."

As if in response to Sadie's prediction, a few more shoppers filtered in.

"I won't keep you, but I have some bad news." Liz lowered her voice, glancing around to be sure none of the women browsing nearby could overhear. "Bob Stevens died last night."

"What?" Sadie dropped her keys on the glass counter with a crash. When everyone looked over, she smiled and waved the keys. "Sorry. I've got butterfingers today." The smile dropped as she whispered to Liz, "That's so sad. What happened?"

Liz stepped closer to the counter and told Sadie the tragic story. "I'm going to call the chief later and find out what the verdict is, if he knows."

"Finding him must have been horrible, and I feel for you. But . . ." Sadie cast a skeptical gaze at Liz. "It's quite a coincidence, isn't it, that both Claudia and Bob faced life-threatening situations within one week?"

Put that way, Liz had to agree. If Sadie was right, then the killer failed with Claudia and succeeded with Bob. What was the motive? Money or something more obscure, like love or revenge? Why now?

Caitlyn bustled in, unwinding a scarf from around her neck as she went. "Brr, it's cold out there. I can't believe it snowed yesterday. And stuck." She lifted one boot. "I've got snow packed in my treads. Way too early for that."

One of the shoppers stopped her as she passed. "Is this the store the poison pie baker owns? Someone said it was."

Her friend nodded eagerly, staring at Caitlyn.

"Poison pie baker?" Caitlyn reared back, obviously caught off guard.

Sadie groaned under her breath, then boomed, "If it means you'll buy something, then, yes, the poison pie baker does own the store. If you're just a looky-loo, then, no, she doesn't."

The inquirer exchanged startled looks with her friend, and both scurried out of the store at full speed. A moment later the front door banged shut.

Sadie chuckled in satisfaction. "That took care of them."

"You're something else," Caitlyn said, joining Sadie and Liz at the counter. "I was totally blindsided by that rude question. I couldn't even form a coherent answer."

"Wait until you're my age," Sadie said. "You'll have seen it all. And heard it all too."

Another customer came up to the counter with a meek smile. "I'd like to buy some cloth off the bolts." She appeared curious, but she held her tongue about the scene she had just witnessed.

Liz smiled to herself. Although bighearted and kind, Sadie knew how to manage people and keep them in line.

"I'll be right over," Caitlyn said to the customer. "Bring what you want to the cutting table." She turned to Liz and Sadie. "Guess what? My car loan is still messed up. I got two payment slips in the mail—from two different places."

Liz frowned, her lawyerly instincts provoked by this information. "Something's wrong."

"That's what I thought," Caitlyn said. "I've got another call in to Stevens' Motors. But you know how it is the day after a holiday. They're probably swamped."

"Keep trying," Liz advised. "If you can't get a resolution, it might be time to have an attorney call. The first loan should have been paid off with the proceeds of the second."

"What a mess." Caitlyn glanced over at the cutting table, where her customer was plopping down bolts of cloth. "I'd better scoot. Talk to you later."

"I'd better get going too," Liz said. "I've got rooms to clean." She needed to change the bed in the room vacated by Tony. Plus, she wanted to freshen up the other bedrooms and baths.

"Feel free to stop in later. I'd like to catch up on everything."

Sadie glanced toward the doorway, where even more customers were entering. "But at this rate, it doesn't look like I'll get a chance until we close at five. At least staying busy will help me keep my mind off Mary Ann's predicament."

"I hear you." As Liz walked out of the store, nodding at customers, she wondered if Bob's death had a bearing on Mary Ann's case—or should. In addition to the possibility that both Claudia and Bob were poisoned by the same hand, there was also the chance that Bob was guilty and had killed himself out of remorse. Once she got her chores done, she'd give the chief a call.

The Greggs were out and about, shopping no doubt, Piper was at her family's farm, and Sarah had the day off, so Liz had the place to herself. Starting on the third floor, she worked her way down, changing beds, dusting, and scrubbing bathrooms. All of it was very therapeutic as well as good exercise.

Liz huffed and puffed as she lugged the vacuum cleaner down a flight of stairs. *I won't need an aerobics class this winter. Who knew housework would work so many muscles?*

The pride of a job well done was another reward, and she allowed herself to admire the neat and attractive rooms before heading to the kitchen for an overdue lunch. She heated up a can of tomato soup and made a grilled cheese sandwich to go with it, then sat at the kitchen table to eat. Outside the window, brilliant sunlight glinted off melting icicles and patches of grass were revealed as the snow receded.

Beans trotted in, snuffling around her feet in search of dropped crumbs.

"Sorry, Beans, none for you. But I'll give you a treat if you wait a minute." Amused at finding herself talking to the dog, Liz chuckled. "I guess it's marginally better than talking to yourself, right, boy?"

Beans sat nearby, panting, his huge tongue flinging drops everywhere.

Liz chose to interpret that as agreement. "Well, your crazy

owner is going to give the police chief a call as soon as I clean up these dishes."

Comically, Beans groaned and flopped flat, head on his paws.

After giving him a doggy snack, Liz went to her quarters to place the call. Even though the guests were out, she didn't want to risk being overheard.

The dispatcher put her right through.

"Hi, Liz. How are you?" The chief's voice was a low, comforting rumble. "I know last night must have been rough for you."

"It was, but I'm all right." Liz paused. "Chief, I can't help but think something is odd about Bob's death."

The chief cleared his throat. "You mean foul play? No, I'm afraid he either accidentally or on purpose took a few too many sleeping pills on top of drinking quite a lot of whiskey. It's sad, very sad indeed, but people don't realize you shouldn't mix—"

Liz pounced on the opening. "That's what the coroner said?"

Houghton sighed. "I really shouldn't be having this conversation with you since the formal report hasn't been released, but, yes, that's what he ruled as the cause of death."

"Let's say that's right. If Bob killed himself, then maybe it was due to guilt over trying to poison his ex-wife."

"I see what you're trying to do, point the finger at someone else, not your friend." He gave a dry chuckle. "I don't blame you, but we can't speculate. And Bob's death doesn't change the case against Mary Ann. For one thing, no one saw Bob go into the kitchen."

"Maybe he was working with an accomplice." Even as she said the words, Liz knew how far-fetched they sounded.

"You're reaching. There's no evidence of collusion with anyone else either. No, I'm afraid the two incidents aren't related."

And I'm almost certain they are. Liz hung up the receiver a trifle harder than she had to. Apparently, it was up to her to figure out exactly what had happened at the Order of the Otter Lodge and at Bob's house. Not that she blamed Chief Houghton. He had to follow the rules, and right now the evidence pointed strongly to Mary Ann. But she refused to believe that Mary Ann had tried to kill someone—or ever would.

That afternoon, the Greggs returned laden with packages and bags. Upon Liz's offer they settled in the sitting room while she put on coffee and hot chocolate. She was pouring water into the coffeemaker when Connie entered the kitchen.

"Liz, I was wondering if you'd do me a favor."

Liz concentrated on not spilling the water before asking, "Sure. What is it?"

"I'm worried about Claudia."

16

"Has something happened?" Liz heard the sharp note of fear in her own voice.

Folding her arms across her chest, Connie began to pace the kitchen. "That's just it. I don't know. I've been calling her house and her cell, and she's not picking up."

"She's not at work." Liz's remark was a statement, since she guessed that Claudia was no doubt still recovering from her ordeal.

"No, of course not. The doctor told her to take a week off." Connie made a huff of exasperation. "And that young woman who works for her—Tiffany, I think—was no help at all. She said she didn't know where Claudia was."

"Maybe she's out of town," Liz suggested. She took milk out of the fridge for hot chocolate made the old-fashioned way, with cocoa powder and vanilla.

"If she is, she didn't mention it when I called her yesterday." Connie paused. "And before you ask, no, I didn't tell her about Bob. I didn't want to be responsible for causing a setback."

"So, back to the favor. What do you need?"

Connie shrugged, smiling ruefully. "I was wondering if you'd go over to her house with me."

A sigh rose in Liz's chest, but she managed to tamp it down—barely. "If I'm the only one who can go . . ." She let her voice trail off, hoping

Connie would take the hint. Then she realized something. Maybe this was a perfect opportunity to learn more about the poisoning incident from Claudia herself. "On second thought, of course I'll go. In fact, I'll pick up a nice plant and take it with us. I should have done that already."

"Great idea." Connie glanced at the clock. "How about in an hour or so?"

Liz agreed, then rushed out to a nearby nursery and bought a Christmas cactus almost ready to bloom. When she got back to the inn, she found Connie, and the two of them got in her still-warm car. "Where to?" Liz asked.

Connie didn't speak for a minute. Then she shook herself. "I'm sorry. I think I was having a flashback to the car ride we took last night to Bob's house."

Me too. "I'm sure Claudia is fine," Liz said. In response, her belly tightened with the knowledge that she could very well be wrong about that.

"I hope so," Connie said. "Turn right. She lives in the historic district."

The historic district was a nearby neighborhood, a network of streets lined with beautiful, elegant turn-of-the-century houses.

"That one," Connie said, pointing to a brick foursquare with a wide enclosed porch and a cupola on top. "She must have inherited the house when her parents passed away. I remember visiting her here when we were kids."

Liz slid into a space in front of the house and shut off the ignition. Dusk was falling, and lights were popping on in the houses around them. But not in Claudia's house. "No lights are on. It doesn't look like anyone is home."

Connie peered up at the house through the car window. "You're right. But I suppose we'd better check." She shuddered. "What if she's in there all alone?"

Dead. Liz reluctantly opened her door and got out, then reached into the backseat for the cheerful plant. They trooped side by side up the brick sidewalk to the porch, which held two rocking chairs. Liz stood back to let Connie go up the steps first.

Connie rang the bell, the sound pealing inside. She paused, then rang again.

No response inside the house.

Liz set the plant down and went to a window, putting both hands to her face to peek inside. Through the open drapes, she saw an empty living room, everything neat and tidy. "It doesn't look like she's home."

Connie's face twisted. "What if she's ill upstairs and can't get to the door?" She tried the knob, but the door was locked.

"Without any evidence to the contrary, we have to assume she's not home," Liz said.

"I hate to do that after what happened to Bob." Connie thought for a moment, then snapped her fingers. "The garage. Let's see if her car is here."

"Good idea." Liz followed as Connie bolted down the steps and hurried down a short path to the driveway. Square and brick like the house, the garage had a line of small square windows in the door, providing a view into the interior—if you stood on tiptoes.

The garage was empty.

Connie dropped to the soles of her feet with a grunt of disappointment. "She isn't home. Let's go back to the inn. Sorry to drag you out here."

"No problem. I guess I'd better grab the plant. It's too cold to leave it on an unheated porch." Liz pushed a button on her key fob, and the car lights flashed. "It's unlocked, so go ahead and get in."

Connie headed for the car while Liz climbed the porch steps again. As she bent to pick up her plant, she noticed a newspaper inside a plastic bag. She glanced at the date. It had today's date, another sign that Claudia wasn't home. Then she noticed something pink behind the closest rocking chair. Still bent over, she moved closer to the object.

One terry-cloth slipper.

Liz couldn't shake off a sense of uneasiness as she drove back to the inn despite her efforts to tell herself she was overreacting. Maybe Claudia had dropped the slipper on the way home from the hospital. Or it had been with a bag of clothes destined to be thrown away or donated, and had fallen out.

She imagined herself calling the chief and telling him she'd spotted a lone slipper on Claudia's porch and they'd better put out an all-points bulletin. The thought of his reaction made her snort.

Connie glanced over. "What is it?"

"Nothing." Liz wiped the inappropriate smile off her face. "Just thinking."

"Me too." Claudia shifted in her seat. "You know how sometimes you lose your temper, and then you feel terrible about it afterward?"

"Yes," Liz said slowly, thinking it was better to encourage her confidences by agreeing. "That happens to everyone."

Connie sighed. "I had a terrible fight with Claudia." She fell silent, staring out the window at the passing houses.

Liz signaled for her street, hoping she appeared calm on the outside even though inwardly she was screaming for Connie to continue. Finally, she said, "Really? That must have been awful." She crept to a crawl, knowing that stopping at home might interrupt the discussion.

"It was awful." Connie turned slightly in her seat to face Liz.

Sensing Connie's gaze on the side of her face, Liz arranged her features in what she hoped was an encouraging expression.

"I was trying to help her, but she blew up at me."

"How annoying." Liz hazarded a guess. "Were you talking about Bob?"

"No, that fight happened years ago. She treated him like dirt, but he seemed to lap it up." Connie gave a sad little laugh. "And look how that turned out."

They had reached the driveway to the inn, but Liz kept going. She'd circle the block, she decided. She hoped Connie wouldn't—

"Hey, isn't that the inn?"

Liz laughed. "Yes. We were having such a good talk I didn't want to interrupt you. Plus, I wanted to check out the neighborhood Christmas lights."

"Oh, that's a good idea." Connie stared at a house gaudily trimmed with white lights on its eaves, doors, and windows. "They are nice."

"So, Connie . . . ," Liz prompted.

"Remember the night of the football game? I ran into Claudia in the bathroom at the high school. I had just learned that Kevin Fiske was her business partner. I couldn't believe she'd ousted Bob for him."

"You know Kevin?"

"Who doesn't? If they'd had the category in our yearbook, he'd have been voted most likely to end up in jail."

Liz was taken aback. "Really? That bad?" She swung the car onto another side street. She had to hear this.

"You bet. He was always in trouble, even got arrested a few times. Those records are sealed now, of course, since he was a minor, but we all knew about it."

"So, maybe he's reformed. That's the point of keeping juvenile records confidential, isn't it? To give kids a second chance?" Liz glanced over to see her passenger sitting with her arms folded and her lips pressed together.

"True. But some kids don't learn from their mistakes. And I think Kevin is one of them."

"Think or know?" Liz kept her tone gentle, not wanting to anger Connie.

"Let's just say I heard it from a very reliable source."

Liz's heart sank. Gossip and hearsay were useless. "What happened after that?"

"I didn't speak to her again until the day of the contest."

The car lurched as Liz hit the gas a little too hard. "Sorry. How did that talk go?"

"We only said hello to each other. She was kind of chilly but cordial at least."

"Did she know you were in the contest?"

Connie shook her head. "I didn't have a chance to tell her."

Didn't have a chance or deliberately didn't say? Liz wanted to take Connie at face value as a devoted wife, anxious stepmother, and concerned friend. But she knew from previous situations that she shouldn't jump to conclusions about someone's guilt or innocence.

"Poor Ron. He was so afraid the police would try to pin it on me since Claudia and I have a history. I told him that's exactly what it was—history."

Liz thought back to Ron's discomfort in the hospital elevator when discussing the case. Was his uneasiness because he feared Connie would be blamed—or did he know she was guilty?

"Can we go back now?" Connie asked. "We're all going out to dinner at Mama's Home Cooking, and I'd like to freshen up."

"Of course." Liz turned onto a side street that led back to the inn. "You'll like Mama's. She makes great meat loaf."

Liz woke up at three a.m., a vision of a pink slipper in her mind. Had she been dreaming about it? Where was Claudia? On vacation or in harm's way again? Her thoughts began to churn, going over every detail of the past week. Poor Mary Ann. She really should call her in the morning and see how she was doing. Her family was so nice, and the grandchildren were adorable. How terrible for them to have to deal with Mary Ann being arrested and potentially on trial.

And what about Bob? So sad. Had he really killed himself? Another memory drifted in. An elderly man, standing on a stoop, watching the police officers and ambulance arrive. If Bob's death was ruled accidental or suicide, then the officers probably didn't bother to question the neighbors.

She would go talk to the neighbor in the morning. Maybe he'd seen something—or someone.

With this decision, Liz felt herself drifting back to sleep. One more thought jolted her awake. Claudia's wrecked car. Someone should take a closer look at it.

She sank into slumber again, this time dreaming that the elderly neighbor was wearing pink slippers.

―――――― //////////////////////// ――――――

In the morning, Liz was at the stove making pancakes when Piper wandered into the kitchen.

"Java," Piper cried, hurrying toward the coffeepot. She laughed. "I'm so sleepy this morning." She picked up the carafe and poured a cup.

"Me too," Liz said, flipping a flapjack. "I had strange dreams all night." She turned the link sausages sizzling in another pan. "How are things with your family?" She'd barely seen Piper the past couple of days.

Piper leaned against the counter and sipped her coffee. "Things are great. As you know, I've been spending most of my time over at the farm." She smiled. "Vater is doing much better. Apparently, the treatments are working."

I think seeing his daughter is the real healing tonic. "I'm really happy to hear that." Liz scooped up three pancakes and put them on a plate. "These are ready if you want them. There's real maple syrup on the dining room table. A friend sent it to me from New Hampshire." She added two sausages to the serving.

Piper straightened. "Yum. I'm starving. Thanks." She took the plate, still holding her mug in the other hand. "By the way, I'm quitting the show and staying in Pleasant Creek for a while."

Liz poured three more circles of batter into the hot frying pan. "Do you need to extend your reservation?" Her heart sang at the idea of an extended-stay guest, especially one she liked.

"A couple more weeks, probably. I'll be looking for an apartment."

"I know some people you can contact about rentals. Let's talk later." Liz made a shooing motion. "Go on and eat before it gets cold."

The Greggs descended for breakfast, devouring stacks of pancakes like locusts, and then they were gone again, out for a ride in the countryside. Tonight was their last night, and Liz didn't have new guests coming until Tuesday. That meant she could take a nice break on Sunday and do thorough room cleanings on Monday when Sarah was due back in. The knowledge that a well-deserved rest was coming made her spirits light as she cleaned up the kitchen and dining room and did the dishes.

The overcast day was only slightly warmer than the previous one, and Liz was grateful for her hat and gloves when she hopped into her car for the ride over to Bob's neighborhood. Her heart beat faster in anticipation of her errand since the outcome was unpredictable. In her attorney days, she'd thrived on controversy and confrontation; now she prayed that Bob's neighbor would be forthcoming. She was all too aware that she was stepping into the police's territory.

Liz parked in front of Bob's town house and surveyed the one across the street. As she hoped, the curtain twitched, signaling the elderly neighbor was home. She got out of the car and locked it, then crossed the street and knocked.

After a minute, she heard the rattle of the knob, and the door opened partway, revealing the slender, neatly dressed man she remembered. "Can I help you, miss?"

"I hope so." Liz paused, wondering how to broach the topic. Then she decided she might as well be frank. "I noticed you the other night when Bob Stevens died." She nodded toward Bob's house.

He took a step back. "I heard the sirens and saw the lights, so I came out. It was only natural."

"Of course. I understand. Anyone would have been curious." Liz took a deep breath. "I was the one who, uh, found him, and I would like to talk to you."

With a nod, he stepped back, opening the door. "Why don't you come inside? It's freezing out here. I can put coffee on if you want."

"That sounds lovely." Liz followed him into the house, which was identical in layout to Bob's.

"What a terrible thing. Bob was about the age of my oldest son." He indicated the sofa. "Have a seat. I'm Clarence, by the way."

"And I'm Liz." She perched on the sofa.

Clarence went into the kitchen, separated from the living room by a breakfast bar. "I have one of those pod things my son gave me to make single servings. Dark or light roast?"

"I'll take dark," Liz said. "With milk or cream, no sugar."

"Coming right up."

Liz gazed around, noting the many photos of two boys close in age. *Where do his sons live?* she wondered. *Is this nice old man alone on holidays?*

Clarence shuffled out carrying two mugs, setting one close to Liz on an end table, then settling in an armchair. It faced the window overlooking the other units, Liz noticed.

They sipped in silence for a moment, and then Clarence spoke. "Was Bob a good friend of yours?"

"Actually, no. But he was close at one time to the woman I was with that evening when we stopped by. They had dated in high school."

"That must have been awful for her." He studied Liz. "What was it you wanted to talk about?"

Here we go. "Bob apparently died of an overdose of prescription pills mixed with liquor. They think it might have been suicide, but I'm having a hard time accepting that."

"Suicide?" Clarence's brow creased in a frown. "That doesn't sound like Bob."

"That's what I thought. Surely, he had everything to live for, including a lot of friends who cared about him." Liz crossed her fingers, hoping Clarence knew something that would lead her in the right direction.

Clarence pursed his lips. "I wouldn't say he had lots of friends, but there were a few." He gave a hoarse chuckle. "Especially lately. He had a real pretty woman visiting him now and then. She even came over on Thanksgiving."

17

Liz's heart lurched. Someone had visited Bob the day he died. "I wonder if I know her. What did she look like?" She tried to keep her tone casual, as if she wasn't fishing for evidence in a murder case.

"A lot younger than him. Dark hair, with a real good suntan. She must use one of those tanning booths." Clarence shook his head. "Not a good idea. They can cause cancer."

"Really? I hadn't heard that." Inwardly, Liz was exultant. Bob's visitor had to be Tiffany Blake. She'd seen them together at the concert, and Tiffany was the only brunette she'd seen around town sporting a suntan in November.

Clarence spoke a few minutes about skin cancer, and when Liz saw an opening, she asked, "What time did the young woman visit? I'm hoping Bob enjoyed a nice Thanksgiving dinner before he . . . you know."

"Me too. It was early afternoon. I didn't see her carrying in a turkey, but maybe Bob cooked." Clarence sniffed. "Us singles have to learn how to do that."

"I know." Liz smiled. "My son is far away too. In Kosovo, as a matter of fact."

The conversation turned to a discussion of their distant sons. She was happy to learn that both his boys would be back for Christmas, families in tow. Clarence promised to have his boys call the inn since they needed a little more room than his two-bedroom town house could provide.

When Liz finally left, she felt truly heartened. Not only had she gained a vital clue about Bob's death, she had made a new friend. She might even have the privilege of hosting Clarence's sons at Christmas.

Back at the inn, Liz popped in to see Sadie. "Let's have an emergency Material Girls meeting tonight after you close. I've got some important updates to share."

Sadie raised her brows. "That sounds intriguing. Caitlyn stepped out for a few minutes, so I'll tell her when she gets back. Do you want to give Mary Ann a call?"

"I sure will. Naomi and Opal too." With a renewed sense of energy, Liz went to her quarters to make the calls. Then she spent the next hour writing down everything she could remember and a list of questions. On paper, her theories looked like speculation, but her intuition told her she was closing in on the truth.

On an impulse, she picked up the phone and dialed Stevens' Motors. Tiffany answered. "Hi there. This is Liz Eckardt. I'm looking for Claudia."

A pause as the sound of shuffling papers was heard. "I'm sorry, but she's not in. May I take a message?"

"Hmm. Do you know when she'll be in? I really need to talk to her." Liz tried to sound both casual and insistent.

"No, I'm sorry. I don't know. She's out sick. I'd be happy to take down your name, number, and the purpose of your call. Maybe the manager can help you."

Kevin? I think not. "I don't think so. This doesn't have anything to do with the dealership." She thought quickly. "Claudia asked me to be on a committee." That sounded plausible.

Tiffany snorted. "Oh yes, Ms. Stevens and her committees. I'll tell her you called."

Liz pressed further. "You don't have a cell number for her by chance, do you?"

"I'm sorry, but I can't give that out. Company rules." She lowered her voice. "Plus, she'll kill me. She hates to be bothered on her mobile."

Too bad. She'd love to call Claudia and make sure she was all right. She was tempted to press Tiffany but decided to wait. It was too easy to avoid questions or lie over the phone.

When the meeting time rolled around, Liz grabbed a tray of cookies and hurried to Sew Welcome. Here she found the others gathered in a circle, working on their quilting project for charity. "How is everyone?" she asked, setting the tray next to a plate of double-chocolate brownies Naomi had brought. "I guess the answer is, in need of chocolate," she said with a laugh.

"I figured we could all use a morale booster," Naomi said. "And those brownies work for me."

"Me too," Caitlyn said. She sighed. "We were so busy all day that my feet hurt. I'm almost as tired as when I work at the hospital."

"I'm glad you could fill in for me. I appreciate it." Mary Ann looked drawn, and even her bob wasn't as shiny and full of body as usual.

"No problem." Caitlyn smiled. "I was happy I had the time off from the hospital."

After Liz settled in a chair, Sadie said, "Fill us in. What have you found out?"

"First, I don't know if all of you heard, but Bob Stevens died." Although Liz had shared the news with Sadie, she hadn't wanted to disturb the others during their holiday celebrations with more bad news.

"Claudia's ex-husband?" Mary Ann's face went white. "That's awful. I've been so busy with my family I haven't even read a newspaper or turned on the television." She frowned. "And I didn't want to read about myself."

"The coverage of Bob's death has been fairly low-key so far," Sadie said. "Probably because of the holiday."

"Wait until the media puts two and two together," Naomi said. "It's tabloid material for sure. A prominent woman is poisoned, and her ex-husband dies a few days later."

"It is really strange," Opal said. "I smell a rat."

"Me too." Liz shared what she knew and how she and Connie had discovered Bob after Connie wasn't able to reach him. "The police think it was an accidental overdose or suicide, but I think it was murder even if I can't prove it yet. And I think Tiffany Blake is involved somehow."

"Tiffany?" Caitlyn sounded puzzled. "I can't believe that. I mean, she used to be kind of a wild child, but she's settled down now. She's even going to college part-time."

"That's right," Liz said. "I saw her textbooks at the dealership. But I'll tell you why I came to that conclusion. First, she was at the contest and had access to the kitchen. Second, she was dating Bob."

The other women exclaimed in disbelief—and disgust on Caitlyn's part.

After that subsided, Liz went on. "I saw them together at the concert at the school. They sat next to Jackson and me. But that's not all. Bob's neighbor saw her visit him on Thanksgiving Day, the day he died."

"I see why you're suspicious," Naomi said, "but it all seems circumstantial. Wrong place, wrong time kind of thing."

"Like what happened to me," Mary Ann chimed in. "I don't even know where Bob lived, so they can't pin that one on me."

"Maybe the chief will realize there's more to the story now," Sadie said. "He should look at some of the people around Claudia and Bob."

"Like my guest. At first I was really suspicious of Connie," Liz admitted. "She and Claudia had a fight I partially overheard at the football game. Connie went to high school with Claudia, Bob, and Kevin. She dated Bob back then and never cared for Claudia, I gathered."

"Wow, what a soap opera. What is it, thirty years later and they're still fighting?" Caitlyn set aside her sewing. "Sorry, but I need a brownie to deal with all this."

The others concurred, and by mutual consent, they stopped stitching and grabbed refreshments.

After they were seated again, Naomi said, "Back to Connie. You really think she's in the clear, Liz?"

She nodded. "I'm pretty sure. For one thing, she didn't have access to the kitchen during the pie contest. That I know of anyway."

"What were they fighting about?" Mary Ann asked. "Did you find out?"

"Connie doesn't like Kevin Fiske, the dealership manager," Liz said. "Apparently, what I overheard was her warning Claudia about keeping him on."

"I'm sure that went over big," Sadie muttered. "If there's one thing to be said for Claudia, it's that she knows her own mind."

The pink slipper flashed into Liz's head. "Actually, I'm worried about Claudia. She took some time off work after getting out of the hospital, but she's not at home. Or at least she wasn't when Connie and I went over yesterday."

"Connie again. That woman gets around." Caitlyn rolled her eyes. "Maybe Claudia went out of town for a few days."

"That's what I think." Liz swallowed. "But I hope it was voluntary. You see, I found a slipper on the porch. And I know I'm being foolish, but it really looked out of place."

"Like she was carried away from her sickbed or something?" Sadie took a bite of brownie and chewed. "You may be overreacting on that one."

"Don't forget someone tried to poison her," Opal said. "And I see Liz's point about Tiffany. She was on the scene both times, she works at the dealership, and she knows all the players really well." She cocked one brow. "In Bob's case, perhaps too well."

"What motive did she have?" Naomi asked. "Why would she try to kill Claudia if she was interested in Bob? They were already divorced. And if she was in love with him, then why kill him?" Her eyes widened. "Unless she's a crazed serial killer."

"Serial killer or not, we're missing something," Sadie said. "Information that would make it all fit together."

The friends sat in silence for a few moments, contemplating the situation while sipping coffee and munching on brownies and cookies.

"Duh." Caitlyn hit her head with one hand. "Remember how Piper and Tony were filming the contest? Maybe they caught something."

"Like what?" Opal asked.

"Like someone going into the kitchen who didn't belong in there," Caitlyn said. "Tony told me they keep the camera on because they never know when they're going to catch something cute or interesting for filler. B-roll, they call it."

"That must be fun to wade through," Sadie commented. "But you're right, it's worth a look—if they kept the footage. Wasn't the show canceled?"

"It was." Liz felt a pulse of excitement. "But Tony left all the equipment here with Piper. I hope she didn't delete the files."

"She's still here?" Naomi asked. "I thought she'd be long gone."

"Under normal circumstances, yes, she would be," Liz said, "but it turns out she's Elmo Mast's daughter. You know, the family that owns the turkey farm. And she's decided to stay in Pleasant Creek for a while."

Opal clapped, beaming. "Another family reunion story? Almost like yours, Liz. How wonderful!"

Sadie shook her head in bewilderment. "Piper Reynolds grew up here? Maybe that's why I always liked her so much when I saw her on TV. I must have subconsciously recognized her."

"She used to be Martha Mast, if that helps," Liz said.

"I remember that family," Opal said. "She has a brother who works at the farm."

"That's right," Liz said. "I bought my turkey from Ezra."

The conversation turned to a general discussion of Thanksgiving menus and family gatherings. Mary Ann was sharing a funny story about one of her grandchildren when Liz heard a distinct woof outside the store door.

"Is that Beans?" Sadie laughed. "It sounds like he wants to come in."

Liz hurried to the door and opened it. Beans nudged his way through and trotted to Mary Ann's chair, where he slumped onto the floor, right on top of her shoes.

Everyone laughed.

"I guess he knows I'm going through a tough time," Mary Ann said, reaching down to stroke his back. "How sweet."

"I'm glad Claudia didn't hit him that day," Caitlyn said. "If it *was* Beans who ran out in the road."

Beans lifted his head slightly at the sound of his name, then dropped it with a huge sigh.

They all laughed again.

"Don't you wish dogs could talk?" Liz shook her head. "But if he is guilty, I'm glad she wasn't too badly hurt."

"Her car was wrecked though." Sadie gestured. "*Bam*, right into that tree."

"You know, I wondered about that accident," Liz said. "She should have been able to stop in time if her brakes were working right."

"Maybe that was the first attempt on her life," Naomi said. "After all, she owns a dealership, so anything she drives should be in tip-top shape."

"My thoughts exactly," Liz said. "I still think someone needs to take a look at that vehicle." An idea trickled into her brain. She knew just the person to call.

18

"Thank you so much for having us. We had a great time." Brooke dropped her suitcase next to the front desk.

"We certainly did," Taylor chimed in. "I hope we can all stay here again soon."

"I'd like that," Liz said. "You're all set, by the way. Your parents paid the bill."

"Really?" Jake sounded surprised. "They didn't have to do that."

"We should do something nice for them," Jessica said. "Do you have any ideas, Liz?"

"Well, you could get them a gift certificate for a restaurant around here, but if they're leaving, I don't know when they'll use it."

"Oh, Mom wants to stay a few more days," Brooke said. "She mentioned a funeral for an old friend or something." Her pretty lip curled, revealing what she thought of that downer.

I guess I'm the last to know about their extended stay. Liz reviewed her reservations sheet. She could move an incoming guest to the third floor . . . Yes, that would work.

"Or how about paying for a night for them?" Liz suggested. "That would be simple."

"Great idea." Jake dug for his wallet, then had to fend off his sister and Connie's daughters to give Liz the credit card. "You guys can pay me back later."

Connie and Ron descended from the second floor soon after for prolonged family farewells. With lots of hugs and kisses, their children were off, back to their lives.

"Liz, I know we were supposed to check out today," Connie said once the door closed for the last time, "but we'd like to stay a few more days if you have room."

Liz pretended to look at her reservations, not letting on she'd been given a heads-up. "You can have until Friday in that same room. After that, you'll have to move since I've got a newly married couple coming in."

"Hear that?" Connie elbowed her husband. "Another loving couple. We'll book until Thursday. Bob's funeral is Wednesday afternoon." Her face sobered, and she blinked back tears. "The whole thing is just so terribly sad."

Ron put an arm around his wife. "Come on. Let's get ready to go to Fort Wayne. I need to do some more Christmas shopping."

Connie brightened. "Christmas shopping? That will be fun."

Liz watched them go upstairs with relief. If they left the inn, then Piper could use the big-screen television in the library to review film footage. She didn't want to risk anyone questioning Piper or realizing what she was looking for.

"This is going to take a while," Piper warned Liz early that afternoon after church. "We have hours of footage here."

"That's okay. As long as it takes." Liz settled herself comfortably in a chair next to Piper, who had set up computer equipment on the long library table and connected it to a large TV in the entertainment armoire. Liz had confided the nature of her research to Piper earlier, hoping the television personality would help her by sharing the footage.

"Like I told you before," Piper said, "I had Tony pan the room whenever he wasn't directly focused on action. He might not have caught anything."

"I understand," Liz said, "but we have to start somewhere. Somebody got into the kitchen and poisoned the pie. And that had to be after round one."

"Otherwise the person wouldn't have known which pies were going on to round two." Piper tapped on her keyboard, bringing up the video file for that day. "How devious."

"In all the hubbub, it would have been easy to slip in and out of the kitchen without anyone really paying attention."

"True, so true. Here you all are." Piper stilled the video to display Liz and the other judges, standing uneasily outside the lodge. Claudia was front and center next to Jackson. "Your mayor is certainly handsome."

Liz smiled. "He is, isn't he? We're quite good friends, by the way."

Piper whistled. "Go, Liz." She sped up the file, whirring past the beginning stages of the contest. Once in a while she stopped to look at a certain frame. "I loved working with Tony. See how he picked out the interesting moments?"

Included were a small child gazing at the pies while holding her grandmother's hand, two judges with heads cocked as they conferred, and a look of anxiety on an audience member watching. One frame showed Caitlyn laughing with Sadie.

"It would have been a great show." Liz's comment was heartfelt. "What a shame that it will never see the light of day."

"Not unless we want to exploit a terrible event." Piper moved the mouse. "And I refuse to do that." She scanned through the rest of the first round, Liz watching with interest as she and the other judges examined and tasted the entries. Her face was very serious as if she were deciding the fate of the world.

Piper slowed to normal viewing speed when Claudia announced the first-round winners. "This is where we need to pay attention." She sat back, crossing her arms. "It's about an hour or so before the second round started."

"That's fine. Shall I get us coffee and cake before we really dig in?" Liz could use the energy boost.

"That sounds great." Piper stopped the action. "Need some help?"

Liz stood up. "No, I'm fine." As she entered the kitchen, her cell phone rang from its perch on the counter. Jackson. "Hey, there. Thanks for calling me back." She had called him that morning and left a voicemail.

"Anytime, you know that. What's up?"

"I have a request that you might think is strange." Liz opened the dishwasher and selected two clean mugs, still warm from the cycle.

He laughed, a deep bellow. "Now I'm intrigued. Go on."

"Does the town use certain tow truck operators to respond to accidents?"

His response was swift. "Are you all right?"

Liz laughed. "I'm fine. I was thinking about Claudia's accident. She wasn't in any shape to call a truck herself."

"In that case, yes, the police call someone. They go down a list and see who they can get."

"Is there any way that, as mayor, you can find out who picked up her car? I really want to get a look at it." Her next task was to slice a coffee cake ring and place the thick, crumbly wedges on plates.

Jackson played along. "I can do that, but it will cost you."

"How much?" Liz set the plates and mugs on a tray, and added forks and napkins.

"You have to tell me what's going on." He chuckled. "I can't imagine what it is."

"I will. I promise. Thanks so much." Liz hung up, still smiling. Maybe he could find out today, even if it was Sunday. It was convenient having friends in high places, so to speak, if Pleasant Creek's city hall qualified as such. She poured coffee into the mugs, grabbed milk and sugar, and picked up the tray.

Back in the library, Piper greeted the snack with enthusiasm. "That cake looks awesome. Did you bake it yourself?"

"I did." Liz put the tray on the table. "My baking skills have really improved since I bought the inn."

Piper picked up her plate and dug in. "Tastes as good as it looks. What did you do before?"

"I was a patent attorney in Boston." Liz shook her head, bemused. "About as far from being an Indiana innkeeper as you can imagine." She gestured at her jeans and sweater. "No more high heels pinching my toes, long hours poring over documents, and demanding clients."

Beans waddled in, tongue lolling, obviously attracted by the scent of cake.

"Unless you count him."

"He looks very demanding." Piper dropped a crumb, accidentally on purpose, and Beans lapped it up. "Oops."

"He'll be your friend for life now." Liz cut into the cake and took a bite. It *was* good, a nice blend of vanilla cake and buttery brown-sugar topping.

"It's good to hear that you successfully made the shift from urban life. I want to do the same." Piper added milk to her coffee. "I'm not exactly sure what I'm going to do, but the high school needs an English and drama teacher due to an unexpected vacancy. I thought I'd apply."

"I'm sure your family would love to have you nearby." Liz sipped hot coffee. "Small-town life isn't for everyone, but I enjoy it."

"I'm ready for a change." Piper stretched out her interlaced hands. "Well, back to work."

Much of the video was fairly boring. The Order of the Otter Lodge ladies set up food, and the audience came up and purchased it. The kitchen door was visible behind the table, and Liz kept her gaze focused there.

Jackson went in and came out, lugging a bowl filled with ice for sodas. The ladies ran back and forth, collecting more food to sell. Claudia disappeared for a while, then sauntered out, sipping a cup of coffee.

"Did you go into the kitchen, Piper?" Liz asked.

Piper paused the video. "For a minute. It's huge. They had the food for lunch set up at one end, where there are a couple of fridges. At the other end of the kitchen is a big walk-in. That's where they stashed the pies. Hang on a second."

She noted the time they were presently viewing and reversed to before the judges arrived. Tony had filmed the kitchen, and Liz could clearly spot the coffee urns and a line of platters on a counter to the right. The camera went along, panning from the huge stoves and sinks to the walk-in fridge. Inside the fridge were several racks lined with covered pies, all with large, bold numbers on cards taped to the containers.

"This is great. We have the crime scene on video." Maybe the police could find some evidence inside the cooler.

Piper appeared startled. "I didn't think of it that way, but you're right." She peered at the numbered pies. "I wonder which ones were Mary Ann's."

Liz thought back to the day of the contest. "Number 38. How could I forget?"

"Here we go." Piper zoomed in closer to the numbers. Number 38 was on the second shelf down in the middle.

Had Mary Ann been specifically targeted, or was her pie doctored because she was one of the finalists?

"Have you seen enough?" Piper asked. At Liz's nod, she made a note of the time stamp, then forwarded to the break between rounds.

"You're really good at this," Liz said, admiring Piper's dexterity at finding the right spot.

"What can I tell you? Lots and lots of practice." Squinting, Piper leaned forward, stabbing at the screen with her finger. "Who is that?" She zoomed in.

"It's Tiffany Blake." Liz watched as the dealership secretary, her slender figure and dark hair clearly recognizable from the rear, strolled toward the kitchen door, casually glancing around, clipboard tucked under her arm. She was gone for about five minutes.

"What do you think she was doing in there? Checking on the entries?"

"She shouldn't have been," Liz said. "They announced which ones were going on to the next round, but they didn't bring the pies out until after lunch." A surge of satisfaction filled her chest. "We need to save that shot. I think we may have found our poisoner in the act."

"I'm glad to see you dressed for the occasion." Jackson gave Liz's jeans, boots, and canvas jacket an approving glance as she climbed into his work truck the next morning. He was wearing a similar outfit, with the addition of a ball cap.

"I couldn't exactly wear my pearls and heels to a junkyard," Liz joked back. "I pictured us crawling through oily dirt and weeds."

Jackson put the truck into gear and looked into the rearview mirror to back up. "That may well be the case. Depending on where they put Claudia's vehicle."

"It's such a shame," Liz said. "Her brand-new car was totaled."

"A tree will do that to a car." Jackson nodded at the scarred oak as they drove past. "No doubt the entire front end was demolished, and if the frame was bent, well, that's all she wrote."

"How was your Thanksgiving?" Liz asked.

The rest of the ride out to the junkyard—or auto salvage yard, as the owner called it—was spent trading family anecdotes about the holiday meal. Jackson had an elderly uncle who always nodded off after the first bite of turkey, but his theory was that the poor fellow was exhausted from being the center of attention for a passel of young ones.

"He's just the coolest guy around, and everyone loves him," Jackson concluded as they reached the facility gate, the rest of the yard hidden by a tall wooden fence running along the perimeter. A sign read, "ACE Auto Salvage, Pat Phillips."

Through the gate, Liz glimpsed autos of all vintages and conditions placed in long, dense rows. It reminded her of an abandoned parking lot.

"Junkyards are the original recyclers," Jackson said as he slowly motored through the gate. "If you look close enough, you'll see a Model T or two out there."

"Really?" Liz scanned the closest cars, which all looked modern to her, while Jackson braked in front of a low cinder-block building, a faded "Office" sign swinging in the breeze. An assortment of trucks and industrial equipment were parked beyond the building.

Jackson shut off the engine. "Coming in or do you want to wait here?"

Liz scrambled for the door handle. "I'm coming." She didn't want to miss anything on this outing.

"Hey, Mr. Mayor," a burly man called from behind the counter as Jackson and Liz entered the building. *Pat* was embroidered on his work shirt, and he wore black jeans. "What can I do you for?"

Liz winced at the corny question beloved of certain men as she glanced around. The office consisted of a small area for customers, and on the wall behind the counter were shelves holding mysterious metal parts. Through a doorway, Liz noticed shelves of inventory and a couple of workbenches.

"I called earlier today about parts for a car." Jackson gave the make and model of Claudia's vehicle.

Pat pointed to the yard. "Like I said, we haven't had a chance to strip it yet due to the holiday, but go ahead and take what you need. You have tools?"

Jackson adjusted his cap. "I sure do. Standard and metric."

The junkyard owner gave him a thumbs-up and winked. "That's my boy. Go for it. Bring whatever you want in here, and I'll give you a fair price."

"Wouldn't expect anything less." Jackson gave him a cocky grin. "In fact, I was hoping for a discount."

"See what you can do about my tax bill, and we'll talk." Pat guffawed, as did Jackson.

The banter of men. Liz never failed to be amused at their good-natured posturing.

At the truck, Jackson opened the back door and pulled out a toolbox and a folding jack, which he handed to Liz. "I should have what I need in here."

"Are we actually going to retrieve some parts?" Liz fell in beside him as Jackson started trudging toward the dumped cars.

Jackson shook his head. "If we find something suspicious, we'll have to leave it in place or else wreck the chain of custody. But I might have to take something off to get to the brakes. We'll see."

Claudia's car was at the end of a row, its smashed hood and front mute testimony to the impact with the tree.

"Ugh." Liz studied the damage, grateful the driver had escaped with very little injury, especially if Beans had been involved.

"It looks awful, doesn't it?" Jackson set his toolbox on the ground and hunkered down on the matted grass. He flipped open the lid and took out a flashlight.

"What are you doing?" Liz set the jack next to the toolbox.

"I'm going to crawl underneath and see how the brake lines look." He got on his back and wiggled underneath the vehicle.

Liz crouched near the tire, hoping to glean information from his muttered comments and grunts. "Find anything?" she finally called.

He wiggled back out from underneath. "Nope. But I'm not surprised. Chief Houghton would have discovered cut brake lines right away." He sat up, then pushed to a standing position, handing Liz the torch before brushing off his pants and shirt. He went to one of the front wheels. "No, I'm thinking it was something a little more subtle."

He grabbed the jack and pushed it underneath the vehicle, then used a bar to raise the front wheel off the ground. A wrench loosened the lug nuts, and Jackson pulled off the tire, revealing the brake assembly. He studied this closely, touching the various parts, then gave a grunt of satisfaction. "I think I found the problem."

19

Liz hurried to Jackson's side and bent to study the brakes. "What did you find?"

Jackson twisted one of the screws on the brakes. "See this? All anyone had to do is loosen these threads and a little bit of brake fluid would ooze out every time Claudia hit the brakes. When she jammed on them to avoid the dog, there wasn't enough left to stop her before she hit that tree."

"They don't loosen up on their own?" Despite Liz's belief that someone had intentionally compromised Claudia's car, she wanted to be cautious.

Jackson snorted. "Not likely. Come on. I'll check the others." He put on the front tire, then moved the jack to the rear. It took a while, but his conclusion was that all four of Claudia's brake assemblies had been tampered with.

"Where do we go from here?" Liz asked Jackson, who started loading his toolbox.

"I'm calling the chief. He needs to know about this." He wiped his hands on a rag, tossed that in with the tools, then fished for his phone. "Hey, Chief, sorry to disturb you on a day off, but that's what you get when you give me your personal cell number." Jackson laughed.

Liz heard a grumbling voice through the speaker.

"Liz and I are at the junkyard, and we just got done looking at

Claudia Stevens's brakes. They were definitely tampered with." He explained how the fluid had leaked from all four brakes.

More grumbling sounds.

"So, basically, the chain of custody was broken, so you can't use the vehicle as evidence? That's just great." Hanging up, Jackson made a sound of disgust. "He said it's going to be impossible to prove that someone at the garage loosened the nuts."

Liz shared his feeling of disgust. "But who else could have done it? Certainly not the tow truck driver or the junkyard owner. Or us."

"We're going to have to figure it out ourselves from a different angle."

"At least we know that the poisoning wasn't the first attempt."

"Unless two different people tried to kill Claudia." His tone was wry. "But how likely is that?"

"Not very. And the Material Girls and I have a pretty good idea who might be responsible." Liz spotted a worker tinkering with a piece of equipment as they trekked to Jackson's truck. "I'll fill you in once we leave."

"That sounds intriguing. I can't wait to hear about it." Jackson hefted the toolbox into the back of the truck, then indicated for Liz to put the jack beside it. "Go ahead and hop in. I'll tell Pat we'll be back later for parts. I hate to do it, but I want to stall him selling anything off that car to someone else before we're done with it."

Liz climbed into the truck. "Good idea. Maybe once he gives it some more thought, the chief will decide he wants to impound it."

Jackson patted his back pocket. "Maybe I'll buy the entire brake assembly and tell them I'll take them off myself so no one else touches it."

"That's generous of you." Liz was stunned at his offer. "But what will you do if we don't need them?"

Jackson grinned. "There are always online auction sites."

Liz watched Jackson stride toward the office. She was very thankful to have him in her corner.

Picking up her handbag, she reached inside for her cell phone and dialed Sadie. "I think it's time to have that beginner's quilting class. With only one student." She smiled. "Tiffany Blake."

———— ** ————

"Gosh, I hope this works." Caitlyn rolled her eyes as she picked up the Sew Welcome telephone. "If it doesn't, what are we going to do?"

"Move to plan B." Liz had no idea what that was exactly, but she'd cross that bridge if they got to it. She gave reassuring smiles to Sadie and Mary Ann, who were watching anxiously.

"Hi, Tiffany. I'm so glad I caught you." Caitlyn's tone was perky. "I have great news." She switched to speakerphone so the others could hear, but kept the phone near her mouth so Tiffany wouldn't catch on.

"Really? What's that?" Tiffany gave an unladylike snort. "I won something?"

"Exactly. You're the recipient of a one-on-one quilting lesson from our very own Sadie Schwarzentruber."

"Sadie? She's cool for an old lady." Tiffany tapped on keys in the background.

Sadie's mouth dropped open, but Mary Ann tugged at her arm, warning her to stay quiet.

Caitlyn grinned at Sadie. "She's very cool. And one of the best quilters in the state. She's won all kinds of awards." Sadie had won a few blue ribbons, but Caitlyn was laying it on thick.

Sadie preened, semi-false credentials or not.

"Huh. So when's my lesson with this famous quilter?" Another telephone sounded in the background. "I can't talk much longer. Phones are ringing off the hook today."

"Actually, that's why I'm calling. We'd like to do the lesson tonight," Caitlyn responded. "Sadie said it's the last night she's available for months. She's extremely popular."

"I don't know . . . I sort of had plans." The phone shrilled in the background again. "Well, I should—"

Caitlyn rolled her eyes again, this time in desperation. Mary Ann glanced at Sadie, then scribbled something on a piece of paper and showed it to her and Liz. Sadie nodded, and Mary Ann gave it to Caitlyn, who gulped.

"If you can do it tonight, then it comes with something extra." Caitlyn paused. "All the materials to make a full-size quilt. That's a really huge value." She named the figure.

"Wow. You know, I really can't pass that up. A private lesson, you said. All right, I'll be there."

Caitlyn gave her the time and hung up, then raised her arms in a victory gesture. "Yes! She's on the hook."

Mary Ann smiled, but her eyes were frightened. "What if this doesn't work? I won't be any better off."

Sadie patted her shoulder. "Think of it this way. If we don't do it, we'll never know for sure if Miss Tiffany is in this up to her pretty little eyeballs or not. We have to start somewhere."

"If you do whatever is in front of you, you eventually get where you want to go." Liz made a face at her own words. "That was convoluted. But you get my drift."

Caitlyn laughed. "I think so. We *have* to question Tiffany. Even if she's innocent, she's connected to the rest of the players." She held up both hands, fingers crossed. "Here's hoping everything goes according to plan."

Tiffany called back right away and tried to cancel, claiming hunger and too much to do at her apartment, but Caitlyn offered to take her out to dinner first. They finally agreed on Mama's Home Cooking at six.

"Drag her over here if you have to," Sadie said. "I've got rope in the Jeep you can use."

"Like a balky calf?" Mary Ann suggested.

"Exactly right," Sadie replied with a decisive nod.

Liz was on pins and needles the rest of the day until she heard the front door open and Caitlyn and Tiffany walk into the inn. She grabbed a plate of mini cheesecakes and a carafe of coffee and hurried into Sew Welcome.

Tiffany was still taking off her coat when Liz entered. She glanced at Liz, then at Caitlyn and Sadie. "This is quite a group for my private lesson."

They'd decided that Mary Ann shouldn't attend due to the pending case.

"Oh, don't mind me," Liz said. "I'm the refreshments committee."

Caitlyn's grin was blinding. "And I'm here to learn and provide support."

Playing along, Sadie pointed at a display of sewing items. "Caitlyn, fetch us cutters, scissors, pins, and a ruler." To Tiffany she said, "Pick out a fabric you like and a couple of others that you think will look good with it."

Tiffany walked over to the array of bolts arranged by color, running a finger along them without quite touching. "Really? Any one I want?" Her eyes were as wide as a child's.

"Yes, any one you want."

Liz felt a pang at the trap they were setting. *But if she's guilty of murder . . .* Liz squelched her softheartedness.

"I like this one." Tiffany pointed to a swirling abstract design in peacock blue and gold. "And this will look good with it, I think." It was a scalloped gold design.

"Good eye." Sadie moved to stand beside her. "How about some contrast?" She selected a striped fabric in black, blue, and gold. With experienced hands, she pulled all three bolts and carried them to the cutting table.

"What are we going to do with it?" Tiffany trailed Sadie.

"Something simple in blocks. We'll start with a small section, and then you can add sections on your own."

Tiffany watched while Sadie expertly cut fat quarters and squares from the three fabrics. She giggled. "I can barely cut a straight line."

Sadie stacked the pieces. "I've had lots and lots of practice. Now on to the next step." She led the way to the workroom, where Liz and Caitlyn were sitting, both working on their charity projects. At the table, Sadie showed Tiffany how to cut a square in half, into triangles, using the ruler as a guide. She handed the cutter to Tiffany. "You try."

With much effort and a couple of false starts, Tiffany managed to cut a square in half, smiling up at Sadie with triumph.

Then Sadie settled Tiffany in a chair with a threaded needle and explained how to stitch two pieces together. "Of course you can always use a machine, but I think it's important to start out by hand so you get a feel for the project."

"I still like to quilt by hand. It's very relaxing." Caitlyn sighed deeply. "It helps me shed all the stress of my job."

"Sounds like something I need," Tiffany admitted. "I go straight to the dealership. If it's not the phones, it's the customers. Or my boss."

"I hear you," Sadie said. "It's hectic here too."

They all stitched in silence for a few minutes.

Then Liz said gently, "I was so sorry to hear about your boyfriend."

Tiffany's head jerked up, and she poked herself with the needle. "Ouch." She sucked on her fingertip. "What do you mean? He's okay as far as I know."

"I was speaking of Bob Stevens." Liz put down her work and tried to appear puzzled. "After I saw you two at the concert, I assumed . . ."

The young woman's face flushed. "Me and Bob? I'd never . . ." She attempted a laugh. "I was sent by Kevin to keep Bob happy. One of my extra job duties."

"That's horrible," Caitlyn said.

"It was all innocent." Tiffany shrugged. "I went on a couple of dates with him; that's all." She pursed her pink-frosted lips. "He wasn't bad for an old guy."

Liz brought the conversation back a step. "Why did Kevin need to keep Bob happy? He wasn't part of the company anymore, was he?"

Tiffany ducked her head, her dark hair swinging forward as she stabbed the needle into the cloth. "He was still part owner. A so-called silent partner." She laughed. "But Bob wasn't all that silent."

"Caused a lot of trouble, hmm? That's too bad."

Despite Sadie's neutral tone, Tiffany flushed again, this time with anger. She scowled. "He wanted to have the books audited. He accused Kevin of skimming, of running a refinance scam." Then she put a hand to her mouth as she glanced at Caitlyn.

Caitlyn dropped her quilt block. "Like he did to me? He supposedly refinanced but never paid off my other loan. Now I owe twenty grand on my old jalopy."

"That was a paperwork error." Tiffany's voice was a squeak. "Honest."

The nurse snorted. "Right. Come on. You know better."

Tiffany's gaze darted around the room, and she rose as though to escape, her stitching sliding to the floor.

Sadie put a hand on her arm. "Sit. You're not going anywhere."

"You can't stop me." Tiffany clenched her fists in defiance, but with a sudden air of defeat, she collapsed into her chair. She burst into noisy sobs, tears flowing as she scrubbed at her eyes, making her mascara run.

"Tiffany, where was Claudia in all this?" Again, Liz deliberately made her voice gentle. She now understood the conflict between Bob and Kevin, but what was the motive to go after Claudia? And where was she, by the way?

The young woman glared at Liz. "That witch? She tried to fire me. She thought I was the one who was . . ."

"Stealing?" Sadie said. "That's what we call it."

Tiffany leaped to her feet and stamped one slender foot. "He was owed all that money. *She* was stealing from *him*! They had an agreement, and she didn't live up to her part of the bargain."

Sadie was unperturbed by Tiffany's antics. "It seems like you care for Kevin. The way you're taking up for him."

"That's because I'm the one he loves . . . not her, not that o—"

"Old woman?" Sadie took another stitch. "She and Kevin are the same age, aren't they?"

"So what? Men don't age like women." Tiffany folded her arms, tossing her head so wildly Liz was reminded of a belligerent horse. And like a tormented animal, Tiffany had been goaded to the point of frenzy. She bolted across the room toward the cutting table.

Caitlyn and Liz exchanged looks of alarm. What was Tiffany doing as she scrabbled around on the table?

Without a word, Caitlyn rose and crossed the room, moving quickly but softly. "What's up, Tiff? Come sit down. You can show me what you've done so far on your project."

Tiffany whirled on Caitlyn, sneering. She held a pair of shears, the point aimed at her friend. "Don't baby me. Everyone always does, and now they're going to pay."

"Who are you talking about?" Caitlyn took a step closer. "Surely not us. We're your friends."

"I don't have any friends," Tiffany snarled, then feinted a blow at Caitlyn, the scissors flashing.

Caitlyn leaped backward.

With gasps, both Liz and Sadie jumped to their feet. Caitlyn made a motion behind her back for them to stay put.

"Put the scissors down," Caitlyn said in a soothing tone. "You don't really want to hurt me."

"Who says?" Tiffany lunged at Caitlyn, scissors held overhand like a knife, and slashed downward.

At the same time, Caitlyn grabbed a bolt of cloth off a nearby rack and held it up like a shield, making the scissors glance off harmlessly. She dodged and sidestepped, swinging the bolt, as Tiffany came on, jabbing left and right.

The opponents parted for a moment, both breathing heavily.

Liz stood frozen, afraid to move and distract Caitlyn. Beside her, Sadie snorted like a steam engine, obviously as frustrated as Liz. Caitlyn's back was to them or else they could use a folding chair to hit Tiffany. There were no other weapons close at hand. Unless . . .

Tiffany roared and leaped toward Caitlyn with renewed fire. Caitlyn swung the bolt but almost dropped it, and the scissors grazed her arm, raising a line of blood.

Caitlyn screamed, and this seemed to encourage Tiffany, who charged her again with a yell, forcing Caitlyn to run backward.

Liz tossed her coffee mug, aiming it to smash on the wood floor right beside Tiffany. The horrendous crash made her pause long enough for Caitlyn to get the advantage. She swung the heavy wad of fabric hard, right into the side of Tiffany's head.

Sadie and Liz jumped into the fray, using bolts to batter Tiffany until she dropped the scissors and curled up into a ball, screaming for mercy. "I'll tell you . . . I'll tell you . . ."

Liz dropped the cloth and snatched up the scissors, chest heaving with effort. When she could speak, she panted out, "Tell us what?"

"Everything. I'll tell you everything."

20

Sadie and Caitlyn grabbed Tiffany by the arms and hauled her to her feet.

Sadie shook the arm she held. "What possessed you to attack Caitlyn that way? She's your friend."

Tiffany's only response was a glare from beneath her tangled hair, which hung over her face. The two women pulled her toward the chairs, and she lurched forward.

"I'm all right." Caitlyn glanced at her bleeding arm. "I want to get this cleaned up right away though."

"I'll get my first aid kit," Liz said. "Don't let her leave."

Sadie and Caitlyn deposited Tiffany in a chair and stood over her.

"Don't worry. We'll stand guard." Sadie gestured at a rack of yarn. "We could always bind her up. Some of that yarn is quite strong."

Tiffany shifted her rear in the seat. "Don't do that. I'll stay put."

Liz was back in two minutes flat, lugging the box of bandages and ointments. Caitlyn rolled up her damaged sleeve, and Liz cleaned the wound, then dabbed it with antibiotic cream.

"Thanks," Caitlyn said, peering at her injury. "I don't think I need a bandage."

"Okay, Tiffany, talk." Liz sat on a chair, gesturing for the others to sit also. They moved their chairs closer into a tighter circle.

The young woman fidgeted, her interlaced fingers wiggling. "I don't know where to start."

"How about at the beginning?" Sadie said dryly. "That's usually a good spot."

Tiffany pouted, her lower lip thrusting forward. "It's all Kevin's fault," she finally said.

Inwardly, Liz rolled her eyes at this blame shifting, but she kept her tone neutral. "What do you mean?"

"Everything was okay until he came along. Oh, sure, Bob and Claudia went through an ugly divorce. That wasn't fun. I used to like Bob until he started drinking too much and making Claudia upset by blowing money. At one point we all thought we might lose our jobs." She paused to sniffle, wiping her nose on her sleeve.

Liz found a clean tissue in her pocket and passed it over. "That must have been rough."

"It was. I have tons of student loans. Our education benefit was one of the first things to go." Her voice rose to a whine.

"So then Kevin came on board?" Liz prompted.

Tiffany crossed her arms. "Yeah, Claudia was all, like, gushing over him and everything. I think she liked him back in school about a million years ago. And the fact that he had bucks didn't hurt either. He bailed us out."

Sadie raised her brows. "Kevin and Claudia were dating?"

"Dating? Heck, no. He hit on me the first day he met me." Tiffany's smile was smug.

Liz pictured the young woman being flattered by the older man's attention, especially if it allowed her to get one up on her disliked boss. Liz sensed Tiffany resented Claudia's status and power.

"Did Claudia know?" Sadie's tone was sharp. "That could be considered harassment."

"No way. I liked him too." Tiffany's eyes lit up briefly. "He's going to take care of me. Guys my age don't have a clue about how to do that." She preened. "Kevin and I are on our way up."

Liz glanced at Caitlyn and Sadie, who seemed equally as concerned and puzzled by Tiffany's shifting allegiances. First she'd been ready to hold Kevin responsible for all her troubles, and now they were a couple again, at least in her mind.

"That sounds exciting," Liz said. "Tell me about it."

"We're going to take over the business. We just need to get old Claudia out of the way. Like Bob." In the quiet room, her words seemed to echo. When the others remained silent, a look of panic slipped over Tiffany's features. "I mean . . . not really *like* Bob."

"It's too late," Liz said flatly. "We caught you going into the kitchen on video to doctor that pie. And now Kevin's got Claudia somewhere, doesn't he?" The image of the pink slipper flitted through her mind.

"What makes you say that? She's at home, resting."

Sadie came down hard on the woman's fear. "Maybe he and Claudia are getting married right now. That'd be the easiest way for him to gain control."

Tiffany shrieked, one hand going to her mouth. "He wouldn't do that. He couldn't, not after all I did for him—"

Caitlyn jumped in. "Your best bet is to help us." She held up her cell phone. "We *are* calling the police."

Wails filled the room as Tiffany tore at her own hair, rocking back and forth. Then the sounds came to an abrupt halt. She batted tear-spangled lashes. "He has her up at the old Stevens' fishing camp."

Jackson floored the truck, making it fishtail on the rutted and icy dirt road. "Sorry," he yelled over the roar of the engine. "This road is in terrible shape."

"No problem." Liz sat braced, one hand splayed against the seat and the other on the dash, silently urging him onward.

After Tiffany told them that Kevin had spirited Claudia up to the isolated camp, she'd clammed up, refusing to say anything else. Liz had a very good idea that Tiffany was guilty of poisoning Claudia and causing Bob's overdose, but there was no firm evidence yet.

Rather than waste precious time waiting for the police, especially since the camp was over the county line and thus raised jurisdictional issues, Liz had asked the others to update Chief Houghton when he arrested Tiffany for assaulting Caitlyn. Now she and Jackson were racing toward the camp with the full knowledge that they might be interrupting a romantic getaway rather than a murder plot.

But if the size of the knot in Liz's stomach was any indication, then the latter was more likely. If someone didn't interfere, Claudia would soon suffer an "accidental" death, of that she was certain.

"There's a split in the road coming up," Jackson shouted. "Watch for it."

Ink-dark trees flew past, not a single light to be seen. They were in the middle of nowhere, far from the civilization represented by a tiny store at the intersection with the state road. Fortunately, Jackson had been out to the camp on fishing trips and knew his way around.

Liz peered into the dark, seeking any sign that their turn was coming up. They were upon it before she realized, the headlights revealing a track hemmed in by thick brush. "There it is!"

Jackson braked, slid to a stop, and backed up; then he nudged the truck onto the side road. "Not many people come down here, as you can tell. There are only a few camps on this road."

Branches grabbed at the truck, some screeching as they ran along the paint, making Liz wince. "This isn't good for your truck."

"I've seen worse." He flashed her a smile, visible in the light from the dash. "You should try an off-road excursion with me sometime." The truck lurched as it hit a pothole, making them both jounce up and down.

"No thanks." Liz smiled back. "I'll stick to roads, thank you."

"You don't know what you're missing." The truck's undercarriage scraped against a rock, and even Jackson flinched. "Maybe you do."

Ahead, their lights illuminated a tunnel through the woods, branches hanging down overhead and undergrowth pressing close on each side. Liz felt a pang of trepidation. What if this was a wild-goose chase? Maybe the couple wasn't even here, and Tiffany was laughing about sending them out into the woods to get stranded. That wouldn't be a joking matter in this weather.

"Jackson. Do you think—?"

Before she could go on, he said, "I know what you're going to say. First, let me reassure you that I've been in this area numerous times and always made it out alive. So no harm done if they're not out here or if the whole thing is innocent. But we have to check."

"Thanks for the reassurance. But I'm surprised that the camp is out here in the boonies. I pictured the Stevens family in a lakeside mansion."

"Old Bob Stevens was a wilderness buff. He liked to get away from it all. The cabin didn't even have indoor plumbing last time I was out there a few years ago."

No indoor plumbing? Not exactly a romantic getaway spot. Once again, Liz wondered if Claudia's journey was voluntary. Liz herself wouldn't be here unless she had to be.

Jackson slowed the truck. "There's one more turn to get to the Stevens' place. I think we might have missed it." He stared out at the overhanging trees. "This doesn't look right."

Liz had no idea how he could tell where they were since the miles of forest seemed interchangeable to her.

The truck lurched along, and then Jackson braked sharply, sending Liz jolting forward and then back against the seat. "I'm so sorry. But look what's ahead of us."

She scooted upright to see over the hood. The rippling black waters of the lake glinted in the headlights. "We almost ended up in the water!"

"I know. The road dead-ends at a boat launch. The water's surprisingly high this year." Jackson put the truck into reverse and backed up into a small clearing to turn around. "The cabin isn't far. The launch actually gave me a landmark to figure out where we are."

"I'm glad it served some purpose besides nearly scaring me to death," Liz said.

Jackson was true to his word. Only a few hundred feet up the road, he turned left into what appeared to be solid forest. But the truck found footing in the rutted grass, and they passed with no difficulty. A short distance in, he switched off the headlights, leaving only the parking lights on. "I don't want to give Kevin any warning that we're coming."

"Won't they hear the truck?"

"I'm going to stop partway up. There's a pull-off we used to park in."

As he located the spot and parked with the truck facing out, Liz was grateful once again that Jackson had agreed to drive her here. She never could have found this place, not in a million years.

Maybe that was the idea. Take Claudia off the beaten track to a location where anything could happen . . .

Jackson turned off the engine and reached into the center console. He fished out two small flashlights and handed one to Liz. "Let's go find out what's going on."

A few minutes later, after a tense and laborious trek across uneven ground in near total darkness, Liz found herself creeping up stairs onto the cabin porch behind Jackson. Lamplight from inside illuminated the center of the deck, so Jackson headed for the wall, where he flattened himself from view.

Liz followed suit. "What now?" she whispered.

He put a finger to his lips before sidling along the wall to the casing framing the double sliding door. He turned his head so he could see inside, then gestured for her to switch places.

The scene that met her gaze was profoundly shocking. Claudia, clad in a pink bathrobe, sat at a table, her legs bound to the rungs of the chair. The normally immaculate business owner looked terrible. Her hair stood up in tufts, and her face was pale and gaunt, without even a touch of makeup.

And she wore only one slipper.

Kevin loomed over Claudia, pointing to the bowl sitting in front of her. He hunkered down, putting an arm around her shoulders and smiling in encouragement. Although his voice was muffled by the glass, Liz gathered the gist.

He was trying to force Claudia to eat. And Liz would bet anything that concoction contained poison or drugs. She clutched at Jackson's arm. "We've got to stop him. He's going to kill her." As she watched in horror, Claudia reached for the spoon with a shaking hand.

"You knock on this entrance," Jackson said, pointing to the sliding door. "I'll go around and come in through the kitchen."

For a moment, Liz quailed at the idea of confronting the murderous Kevin. "What should I say?"

"Tell them there's an emergency at the dealership and Tiffany sent you. By the time they absorb that, I'll be inside." He gave her a gentle push. "Go on. Quick."

Heart in her throat, Liz stumbled into the square of lamplight. Behind her, she sensed rather than saw Jackson slipping off into the night. She breathed in deeply, then raising one fist, rapped on the glass.

Claudia's head jerked around, and the spoon clattered onto the table, sending liquid flying.

With an oath, Kevin rose from his crouch and sprang toward the door. He fumbled at the latch and finally got it open. His eyes narrowed. "Liz Eckardt, what are you doing here?"

"It's an emergency." Liz bit her lip to stop its trembling. "The dealership. It's . . . it's on fire. All the cars are burning."

Kevin stared at her in horror, disbelieving.

"Tiffany sent me. She told me how to get here."

Kevin spun around with an exclamation of rage, snatching up a cell phone from the table. Scowling, he stared at the display, punching buttons. "No service," he snarled and hurled the phone at the stone fireplace, where it hit and fell to the hearth with a *clunk*. He began to pace, gesturing in frustration and confusion. "I'd better get back to Pleasant Creek right now—"

Claudia, who was strangely placid and had barely reacted to Liz's arrival, picked up the spoon and scooped up another serving. As she carried it slowly to her mouth, Liz bolted forward. "No! Don't eat it."

That got Kevin's attention. "What do you think you're doing?" He leaped to intercept Liz, who evaded his grasp, Kevin's hand sliding off her coat sleeve.

As she knocked the spoon out of Claudia's hand, the door in the kitchen crashed open with a *bang*.

Kevin, torn between going after Liz and investigating the sound, stood in the middle of the braided rug, indecisive.

Jackson appeared in the doorway. After noticing the fierce expression on his face, Liz also saw that he was carrying a tire iron. *When had he picked that up?*

"It's over, Fiske."

A look of consternation passed over Kevin's face, but then it vanished, replaced by mocking condescension. "Who are you to bust into a man's house and make threats?" He drew himself up, puffing out his chest. "I'll see you thrown out of office."

"Good luck with that," Jackson said. "I'm having you arrested for attempted murder."

Kevin put up both hands. "Attempted murder? How ridiculous." He threw a nervous glance toward Claudia. "My girlfriend and I were enjoying a quiet evening alone when you two forced your way in."

"Do you always tie up your girlfriends?" Liz asked crisply. Then she couldn't resist. "Maybe that's so they won't run away."

Despite his stern demeanor, Liz thought she saw a flare of appreciative laughter in Jackson's eyes.

"Enough. I've got something to take care of, so get out of my way." Kevin strode forward, arm outstretched and ready to push Jackson aside. "My business is on fire." Then his steps faltered. He looked over his shoulder at Liz. "Wait. You were lying, weren't you?"

"Yes, I was." Liz crossed her arms. "All for a good cause."

The distraction gave Jackson enough time to brace himself in the doorway. "As I said, Fiske, you aren't going anywhere." He swung the tire iron against his palm, as if testing a baseball bat. "We can do it the easy way or the hard way, your choice."

Kevin naturally chose the hard way. Lowering his head, he charged Jackson like a bull. Although the other man was taller and had more bulk, Jackson managed to shove him back. Lifting the tool, he tapped Kevin on the head hard enough to bring him down but not knock him out. He fell flat, groaning.

"The police are on their way," Jackson said, standing over Kevin like a hunter who had downed a moose. "So listen to me this time, will you?"

Claudia clapped. "Bravo. I was wrong about you, Jackson Cross. You *do* deserve to be mayor."

———————— ///////////////////////////// ————————

"All's well that ends well." Sadie lifted a glass of cider in a toast. "To Liz and Jackson, our heroes!"

The other Material Girls sitting around Liz's dining table followed suit with cries of, "To Liz and Jackson!"

In the corner stood one of the Christmas trees Liz had decorated, with others in the rotunda and sitting room, plus a tiny one in her quarters. Electric candles stood in each window, their warm glow evoking the spirit of merry Christmases past in the venerable manor.

"You and Caitlyn are heroes too," Liz said. "Without your help, we never would have learned the truth about Tiffany. And Caitlyn was even wounded in the effort."

Caitlyn lifted her sleeve with a grimace, although after a week the cut was well on its way to being healed. "Only a scratch, as they say in the movies. In this case that's exactly right."

At Liz's lead, the toast went around for Sadie and Caitlyn, then one following for Opal and Naomi and, of course, for Mary Ann.

"You are the epitome of grace under pressure, my dear," Sadie said to her friend. "If I'm ever arrested for murder, I hope I'll handle it as well as you did."

Mary Ann cocked her head, bob swinging as she regarded Sadie with amusement. "I hope you never are. I wouldn't wish it on my worst enemy." She smiled. "I have to admit the spa stay helped me recover very nicely." The Material Girls had gifted Mary Ann with a two-day retreat. "And all the prayers, of course."

"I'm still praying for Tiffany and Kevin," Opal said, her kind face creased in concern. "They really went off the rails, didn't they? And all for greed."

Tiffany and Kevin had been arrested for conspiring to commit Bob's murder and Claudia's attempted murder. Each blamed the other for the decision to permanently remove the obstacles standing between them and complete control of the lucrative business and the refinancing scam.

"Kevin always envied Bob," Sadie said, "and when he saw a chance to swoop in and steal everything, he did it."

"Poor Claudia was just a pawn." Naomi pressed her lips together. "I feel so sorry for her."

"I think she's starting to see that wearing a hard shell doesn't make you invulnerable," Mary Ann said. "She signed up for beginner quilting classes, and she had a blast at the first one."

"She and Miriam Borkholder were laughing their heads off," Sadie said. "It was good to see that."

Liz imagined the scene. Miriam was gifted at putting even the most difficult student at ease. Glancing around the table, she saw that everyone had practically cleaned their plates. She picked up the decimated platter of sliced turkey. "Anyone want more? I can get it from the kitchen." Met by groans and exclamations of being too full to move, she set the platter down with a smile. "On to dessert then." More groans.

"That turkey was from the Mast farm?" Opal asked. "I'll have to start going there."

"Yes, it was." Liz smiled. "I was happy to find out they reserve a few for those who enjoy turkey after Thanksgiving."

"Speaking of the Masts, how is Piper?" Mary Ann asked. "I heard she helped solve the mystery with the video, and I'd love to thank her."

"She's staying here for another week," Liz said. "Then she'll be moving to an apartment. She took a teaching job at the high school."

"That's exciting—for the students," Naomi said. "The town must be thrilled to get a teacher with her experience and background."

"She's happy too." Liz recalled Piper's excitement when she told her about the job offer. "She told me they're going to film an original play one of the students wrote. She's going to take them through the process of creating a movie from script to release."

"Wow." Caitlyn's eyes were wide. "Maybe it will be shown in theaters."

"Probably, at least locally," Liz said.

"Who's ready for my special pumpkin pie?" Mary Ann asked. "The one that almost won an award."

Opal adjusted her glasses. "You're baking that again?" She exchanged openmouthed looks with the others, who also realized that this was a sign of healing.

Mary Ann stood tall, smoothing her skirt. "I sure am." She grinned. "But no whipped cream, now or ever."

The sound of squealing brakes came from the street.

Oh no, not again. Liz glanced under the table. Beans was nowhere in sight. She followed the others to the front door to see what was going on.

A car sat askew, half on the curb, inches from a fire hydrant. The driver's door opened, and a man climbed out.

"Are you hurt?" Sadie called.

"No, I'm fine." He pointed to the inn lawn. "I barely missed that darn dog. It ran right in front of me."

A thin, spotted dog with no collar was prancing around the yard, investigating everything.

"I almost hit him once or twice too," Mary Ann said.

Relief surged through Liz as Caitlyn ran to corral the stray. That dog must have caused Claudia's accident.

She heard panting behind her and turned to see Beans waddling down the porch steps. He flopped to the walk at her feet and gazed up at her as though to say, "You really didn't think it was me, did you?"

Liz bent to stroke his head. "No, Beans, I was sure you were innocent."